Re-disco... kind of story

YOUNG MAN ON A BICYCLE

AND
THE GOLDINI BATH

Victor Canning

This edition published in 2020 by Farrago,
an imprint of Duckworth Books Ltd
1 Golden Court, Richmond, TW9 1EU, United Kingdom

www.farragobooks.com

By arrangement with the Beneficiaries of the
Literary Estate of Victor Canning

'Young Man on a Bicycle' first published in *Cosmopolitan*,
October 1955
The Goldini Bath' first published in *Everybody's*,
October 1956

Print ISBN: 9781788422734
Ebook ISBN: 9781788422727

Have you read them all?

Treat yourself again to the first Victor Canning novels –

Mr Finchley Discovers His England
A middle-aged solicitor's clerk takes a holiday for the first time
and meets unexpected adventure.

Polycarp's Progress
Just turned 21, an office worker spreads his wings – an
exuberant, life-affirming novel of taking your chances.

Fly Away Paul
How far could you go living in another's shoes? –
an action-packed comic caper and love story.

Turn to the end of this book for a full list of
Victor Canning's early works, plus – on the last page –
the chance to receive **further background material**.

Contents

Young Man on a Bicycle

THE young man on the bicycle was very happy. Life was good and the day was fine. The sky above the blue Mediterranean was cloudless, the heat from the sun was making the seed pods of the broom on the red cliffs crack and pop, and away ahead of him on the coast road he could just make out a white sprawl of villas that rose from the harbour of the town where he meant to spend the night. Yes, today life was good. Tomorrow …? Well, if by tomorrow the last of his few francs had been spent on dinner and a night's lodging he, Paul Langley Ashcroft, had no doubt that something would turn up.

Paul was a pleasant-looking young man, with an engaging face that creased naturally into a smile, the kind of face that invited confidences and inspired trust, and he was well aware that it was his most valuable capital asset … that and a ready tongue. He wore a straw boater, cocked Chevalierfashion, a neat grey suit, and a bow-tie as bright as a tropical butterfly. Strapped to the carrier of his bicycle was a large suitcase and various oddly shaped parcels, while along the cross bar were tied an umbrella and a silver-headed walking stick. From the handlebars dangled two straw-covered flasks of wine. The bicycle and the parcels were all rather dusty, but Paul himself looked bright and fresh. Dust found it hard to settle on him. As he rode he whistled and now and again he made little swerving motions across the road as though he needed the extra exercise to release his exuberant energy. The tune Paul whistled was *The World Owes me a Living*. This was his philosophy—and it was surprising how easy he found it to make the world pay up. His methods, of course, were questionable—but the money came. He used what he wanted for himself—and then gave the rest away to those to whom the world also owed a living, but who hadn't got the same grasp of economics as himself. And when the money was all gone, he took to his bicycle and moved on to fresh enterprises as he was doing now.

The road began to dip downhill towards a little cove, its white strip of sand fringed by tall, red-trunked pines. Paul put his feet on the handle-bars and coasted. Half-way down the hill and facing the sea was a large villa, a great pink and white wedding cake of a place, hedged around with black and gold ornamental railings, cut into cool; cypress-studded terraces ... towers, balconies, tiled loggias and, out of sight at the moment, no doubt a private beach. The whole thing was an expensive monument to bad taste. Paul regarded it lovingly. He had long ago decided that. if you were interested in money you had to shut your eyes to bad taste.

The main gates fronting the road had stone columns stuck all over with lozenge-shaped tiles and were surmounted by two figures of bearded seagods holding forked spears and sitting uncomfortably on curled fish-tails. Picked out in gilded letters across the ornamental gateway were the words *Villa Triton*. To one side of the gate was a large wooden noticeboard. Paul put his feet down and braked gently to a stop. Resting his feet on the ground he read the notice and the whistling died from him. For a moment his face was quite solemn, then the sparkle gleamed in his eyes again and slowly the whistle came back ... a fat, rich contented whistle.

The board announced that the villa was To Let Furnished. The agents had their offices in the town on the far side of the bay.

The bicycle rolled on down the hill. Two hundred yards beyond the villa a little wood of pines and tall heather ran up the hillside. Paul dismounted and, with a quick look up and down the road, pushed his bicycle into the trees. He found a sheltered dip crested by heather and began to unpack his suitcase. The first thing he took out a square of mirror with a loop of string round it. He hung this on a pine branch and studied his face carefully in it, running one hand over his fair hair as he did so ... It was a good face, honest, healthy and, when he wished, capable of a hint of gentle melancholy which wealthy, middle-aged women found irresistible—to their cost.

But for the time being, he decided, it was a face which had to be hidden. He began to unpack the rest of his things from his suitcase and unshipped the silver-headed cane from the bicycle crossbar. And as he worked he whistled, but it was now the low, absent whistle of a man who is thinking and planning hard.

When the gate-bell rang Madame Fouret was taking her siesta on the chaise-longue in the housekeeper's room, a pleasant, cool room that overlooked a small side garden where a fountain splashed musically into a great alabaster bowl. She frowned and let it ring twice in the hope that the caller would go away. The gardener was out for the afternoon and she had no desire to answer the gate herself. The bell went on ringing and reluctantly she stood up. She was a tall. angular woman with a pale white face and tight-drawn black hair. She had the eye of an eagle, the mouth of a slave driver, and a heart that pulsed with romantic yearnings the moment she came into contact with any man over forty-five. Dressed in black, her keys swinging at her waist, she went through the house and out into the heat-struck garden like a tall harpy ready to hurl the bolts of her fury at any frivolous intruder.

Within five minutes her heart was captive and pulsing pleasingly. Standing at the gate was an elderly monsieur of the most dignified appearance. He wore a beard and a little waxed moustache. A pair of friendly blue eyes twinkled at her. His voice was cultured and deliberate as be half-bowed and said, "Madame, *chère Madame*, a thousand apologies for disturbing you at this uncivilised hour of the afternoon. But my good friend Monsieur Reynaud—" For a moment the silver head of his cane was tipped towards the agent's name on the notice board, "insisted that I came immediately ... but immediately." He looked up at the villa, "What a charming place, a pearl ... It is for something like this that I have been looking ever since my dear wife died ..." Just for a second the blue eyes under the bushy eyebrows were on Madame Fouret, warm and understanding and with a hint of melancholy in them.

"You wish to look over the villa, monsieur?"

"Monsieur Durobat, madame." The bow this time was a little stiffer, more formal and very impressive, and Madame Fouret was noticing the little button of the *Chevalier de la Legion d'honneur* in the lapel of the well-cut silk suit, the pearl pin in the black stock at his throat, the spats and the wellbrushed velour hat. An industrialist, retired, she wondered ...? Maybe a wealthy professor, a savant ...? But no matter what, a man of presence. His accent was not Parisian. There was a trace of something that she could not place in it. Maybe a retired Colonial administrator ...? But whatever he was she became putty in his hands.

She escorted him into the villa, showed him round, stood by while he admired pictures and porcelain and silently commended him for paying as much attention to the conveniences of bathrooms and kitchens as he did to works of art. When they had exhausted the villa she took him round the gardens. Where the terrace steps were steep he gallantly offered her his arm and for a while she almost forgot that she was merely the housekeeper of the Comte d'Auxier.

Before he went she made a tisane for him and they drank it by the fountain outside her room, talking together easily, as though they had long been friends. By the time Monsieur Durobat left the villa he knew a great deal about its owner Comte d'Auxier and about Madame Fouret. The Comte d'Auxier was in Paris and due to leave for America in a few days. And Madame Fouret, he learned, had only been housekeeper in the villa for the last four years.

Monsieur Durobat refused to let Madame Fouret come with him to the gate. "You have already exhausted yourself too much on my behalf, *chère madame.*" He leaned forward, took her hand and kissed it. "*Au revoir …*"

Monsieur Durobat walked down the hill towards the cove and he was careful to be well out of sight of the villa before he entered the little wood and returned to his bicycle.

Two hours later Paul Ashcroft suitcase in hand walked up the wide steps of the Hotel Argenta and booked a room for the night. By going without dinner he reckoned that he would have just enough money to start operating.

At seven o'clock he put a call through to Paris from his room. He lay on his bed while he waited for it to come through and he was relaxed and happy and whistling gently to himself.

A gruff voice at the other end of the line said, "*Bar des Sports*."

"I want to speak to Felix," said Paul.

"He is busy."

"Tell him to stop playing cards. This is Paul—"

"Ha … Paul. *Mais, oui …*"

A little later another voice said, "Then you are not in prison, Paul? They tell me from Perpignan that—"

"They tell you a lot of nonsense, Felix. Now listen, Felix, I want you to do something for me."

"Anything but lend money. With money Paul you are hopeless. *Diable*, the luck you have but always you get rid of your money stupidly. It is a pity about your father …"

"What's my father got to do with this?"

"Your mother she was French, and your father English. *Mon gar*, it makes the pattern. From her you learn the value of money, but always from your father's side you find ways of being foolish with it. Anything but money I do for you."

"I don't want money. I want two telegrams from Paris. You'll sign them both as the Comte d'Auxier. Send one to Madame Fouret here at the Villa Triton—"

"She is young, good-looking, wealthy?"

"No."

"A pity. For the day you really fall in love I wait. That day you do something extraordinary. I have envy to live to see it—"

"Felix, listen to me. You talk too much. Send a telegram to Madame Fouret saying that you—as Comte d'Auxier—have withdrawn the Villa Triton from the market and have lent it to an English friend of yours, Monsieur Paul Ashcroft, for the summer. He arrives tomorrow."

"And the other?"

"Exactly the same only to the house agents here …" Paul dictated the addresses to Felix, and then went on, "And keep all this to yourself, Felix."

"But certainly, Paul. And this time try and save the money. You are clever, but always you end up with a bicycle and a suitcase. What kind of future is that?"

"Go back to your game and leave the future to me."

Paul rang off. For a moment as he lay back on the bed and stared at the ceiling his face was solemn. People worried too much about the future. That was all right when you began to get old around thirty-five, but at twenty-eight the present was the important thing, the fat, rich, happy present. The solemn look went from his face and he grinned. At this moment of the present he was hungry.

He went down into the wide, expensive reaches of the hotel and found the American Bar. He ordered himself a glass of mineral water and, quite unmoved by the barman's disapproval, began to make a meal from the olives, potato crisps and cheese snacks. The pickles he left alone. They always gave him indigestion.

After a while an elderly man and woman came into the bar and ordered two dry martinis. They were Americans and the man wore a hand-painted silk tie showing the Seven Wonders of the World.

And then, when Paul was just starting on his second dish of potato crisps, another person came into the bar ... Paul, who was a very susceptible young man, fell in love with her at once. Now this wasn't surprising. Women, he considered, were the most wonderful creatures on earth and it was not unusual for him to fall in love three or four times a day. It was a harmless exercise and he seldom did anything about it. His heart would just give a quick bump and a feeling would spread through his body as though he had just swallowed a glass of brandy in a hurry. But with this girl it was rather different. His heart gave a louder bump than usual and he felt as though he had swallowed a large glass of *pernod* without water. Sensibly he put the exaggerated sensations down to a tiring day and an empty stomach.

She was French. As she ordered a glass of tonic water from the barman her voice made this clear. And she was hungry and short of money. This Paul realised from the manner in which the barman served her and the despairing roll of his eyes as she, too, began to make a free meal from the bar savouries. In the old days, thought Paul, one went to a monastery for a free meal and hot soup, but nowadays the American bars of the de luxe hotels were the great dispensers of charity. He smiled at the girl as he caught her eye. She looked through him coldly for three seconds and then turned away. He shifted a little on his seat as he weathered the second impression of a neat *pernod* coursing through him.

Wonderful, he thought; a wonderful creature a neat, pretty little head, crowned with loose black curls, a brown healthy skin, a flash of scarlet lips, the most beautiful, halfbare shoulders over which she wore a green silk scarf, and a body that was sheer poetry... 'She walks in beauty like the night...' quoted Paul to himself and noticed that she had a small run in her left stocking. It made the picture perfect for him. A moment later as she reached out for a dish of olives she knocked her large handbag from the bar counter to the floor. Paul and the American with the tie started for it, but the American won. Normally Paul was a fast starter and could have beaten the middle-aged American easily, but this time he was a little slow off the mark because he was wondering why the girl had knocked her bag deliberately to the ground. He soon knew.

As the American placed the bag back on the counter, saying, "Your bag, mademoiselle ..." it toppled over and, being open from the fall, a small bronze statuette fell out.

The girl said, "Thank you, monsieur," in English and stood the statuette up on the bar. It was a figure of the greek god Hermes.

"Gee, that's cute. Isn't that cute, honey?" said the American's wife who, with the sharp instinct of all women, had come round his flank and was now edging between him and the girl.

"You like it?" The girl was smiling at them. Her accent when she spoke English, Paul decided, improved the language.

"Sure do, mademoiselle. Why it's a perfect little thing."

"It's lovely, *n'est-ce pas*? He was the god of science and commerce and the patron of travellers …" the girl's hand caressed the statuette lovingly for a moment. "One of the fishermen here brought it up in his net … It happens you know from time to time. So many Roman galleys were sunk off this coast in the ancient days. I'm very fond of my little god …"

But not so fond of him Paul knew that she wouldn't be prepared to sell him. And in about five minutes she had for thirty dollars … "A real, genuine antique from the bottom of the Mediterranean. Gee, honey, that's sure something."

When the Americans had gone into the dining room, the girl stayed on for a few moments at the bar while the barman changed her dollars into francs.

Paul caught her eye. Something was wrong with him. Normally when he was in love he was content to worship from afar. Now he felt he wanted to draw closer.

"A beautiful little figure, mademoiselle," he said smiling, his eyes going over her. "But also you should have told them that he was the patron of rogues, vagabonds and—"

"There is no need for monsieur to improve my classical knowledge." She gathered up a bundle of francs from the barman.

"But of course, mademoiselle … there is nothing about you that needs improvement…"

She gave him the beginning of a frown, changed it to the beginning of a smile and then decided on the frown. Pursing her lips a little she said, "*Zut!*" and walked out of the bar.

Charming, delicious … Paul's heart gave a couple of loud bumps and heady with strong emotion he said to the barman, "Who is she?"

Rather stiffly the barman answered, "Monsieur, I do not discuss the people who take free meals at my bar. For me they do not exist."

Paul arrived at the Villa Triton at three o'clock the next afternoon. He had hired a chauffeur-driven car for the week. He had two suitcases in addition to his own which he had bought in a junk shop and stuffed with old papers and a few heavy stones, and a large bunch of dark red roses which he presented to an unwelcoming Madame Fouret. She was stiff and prim and full of disappointment. Only that morning, because of this young English friend of the Count's, Monsieur Durobat had telephoned to say that he would not be taking the villa after all as he understood from the agents that the Count had withdrawn it from the market. She herself had received a telegram confirming this early that morning.

"The roses, madame, are for you," said Paul presenting them to her. "When I left the Count after he had so kindly, and so generously offered me the villa for the summer, he said, "But above all you must look after Madame Fouret well for me." He has a great affection for you, madame. So I ask myself what is the first step to a woman's heart—and the answer is roses. You like roses, I hope?"

Madame Fouret did and she felt herself soften a little towards him as she took them. Only yesterday talking in the garden about flowers with dear Monsieur Durobat she had confessed that dark red roses were her favourites.

"You are very kind, monsieur," she said.

She didn't thaw right away but the signs were there and Paul was in no hurry. He had all the summer before him. She showed him round the villa and from his knowledge of the place he was able to pretend that he had stayed there before. Finally she left him in the Count's bedroom, a wide, airy room with a balcony overlooking the private beach, a room with a great bed shaped like a conch shell and hung with blue silk curtains, a room with a soft blue carpet into which the feet sank with an expensive gasp of surprise.

Before she went Madame Fouret asked, "You will dine here tonight, monsieur?"

"No, madame: I have friends in town with whom I dine. Tomorrow we will talk about engaging more servants. I have many friends in the district and shall entertain a little, you understand. But everything will be left to you. The Count assures me that in your hands these matters are accomplished to perfection ... You would not, I suppose, madame, consider leaving the Count's service and coming with me to England at the end of the summer?"

"Oh, monsieur ... that is not the way to treat your friendship with the Count ..." Madame Fournet laughed, but the compliment was like the first warmth of a liqueur inside her. He was young, and English ... so much against him ... and he had deprived her of Monsieur Durobat ... but even so, she liked the way his eyes sparkled and the deference he paid her. Given another twenty years and he would have been perfect.

"For a pearl like you, madame, I would jeopardise any friendship. Look at this villa so beautifully kept ... One only has to walk into the place to understand that the Madame Fourets of this world are rare ..."

When she was gone Paul unpacked his own suitcase. He owned the suit he wore, an evening dress, and a pair of white flannels and a blue blazer, and, of course, Monsieur Durobat's Outfit. This last, he locked away in one of the other cases.

He borrowed a swimsuit and a beachrobe from the Count's wardrobe and went down to the sea. He sunbathed for an hour and, if he had been a cat, he would have purred. Things were going well, and he knew that Madame Fouret would give him no trouble. Coming up from the beach he wandered quietly through the villa in his beach rate. Comte d'Auxier was obviously a very wealthy man. Paul went through each room price tagging its contents with an acumen any insurance assessor would have envied. When he eventually reached his bedroom the large pockets of the beach robe were full of small, but valuable articles which Madame Fournet would not immediately miss ... four silver ash trays, a tiny jade Bhudda, a silver inkstand, and a little miniature of Marie Antoinette painted on ivory ... As Paul with great care wrapped and packed them all into a parcel he totalled their value ... with luck four hundred thousand francs. That, he told himself, would be enough to set the ball rolling, that and luck, and only a fool ever questioned his luck.

He took a shower and changed leisurely into his evening clothes as the dusk came idly in across the sea turning it to a dark ultramarine. The air through the open window was full of the scent of syringe, jasmine and oleanders and a few fireflies were dancing under the branches of a pomegranate tree. He stood at the window taking it all in, and the odd thing was that for a while he almost felt that he really was Paul Ashcroft the friend of Comte d'Auxier, that he had a right to be here … that he really was a wealthy young Englishman whose father owned a boot-and-shoe factory in the Midlands as he had hinted to Madame Fouret … The only thing missing was someone to share it all … someone young, with dark eyes, red lips and a head of black curls … he sighed. For about twenty seconds he almost regretted having to invent his own fictions and live them. The sight of the paper parcel on his bed brought him back to himself. He picked up the house telephone and asked Madame Fouret to tell the hired chauffeur to bring the car round.

He drove into town sitting next to the chauffeur. Paul preferred always to talk to people, rather than to be on his own. He had an enormous curiosity about them … especially those who suffered from the unimaginative system of economics against which he had rebelled. Already he knew that Madame Fouret had a sister in the town who was convinced. that a month's treatment (alas, too expensive even to be considered) at Aix-les-Bains would cure her rheumatism. And from the chauffeur he learned now that his son's ambition was to study music at the Paris conservatoire ... ambitions, dreams, fading hopes ... people were full of them.

The lights were on along the waterfront, looping away like a great line of coloured beads, the front of the Casino was floodlit, and an idle, happy evening crowd eddied gently across the road.

He had the car stop outside a rather dingy looking jeweller's shop.

As he went inside there was a girl standing at the counter talking to the shopman.

He heard her say, "All right, ten thousand, but you are a rogue and I hope at supper tonight your bad conscience gives you indigestion."

He knew the voice and he knew the girl. Even in me gloom of the shop the black curls shone. He drew back into the shadows as the jeweller answered:

"Good business and a bad conscience, Mademoiselle Elise, they go together. As for indigestion I have been a martyr to it for twenty years. Ten thousand francs for your ring, and if you wish to buy it back at any time you can have it for eleven."

"*Monstre! Avare!*"

From her, Paul decided, the words were compliments, and he saw the old man smile as he passed her money over. As she turned towards the door Paul—a sense of delicacy was strong in him—pretended to study some coffee cups in a case, his back to her. When she had gone he went up to the counter and spread the contents of his parcel before the jeweller. Elise, what a name. It described her perfectly ... Elise.

"Her other name is Benoit, monsieur, and for the next hour she will be taking her supper at the *Dauphin Vert* which is a little cafe five hundred yards beyond the Casino ..."

Paul looked at him in astonishment. "Did I say her name aloud?"

"You did, monsieur ... But I do not blame you. You are at the age. Now what have we here?"

He was a bent-up little man who looked as though he had spent most of his life trying to bore a hole through the top of his breast bone with his chin. He examined the things Paul had brought carefully.

"To sell or to pawn?"

"To raise a loan, papa, for a few days."

"Two hundred thousand."

"Really, papa..." Paul shook his head sadly. "The little miniature of Marie Antoinette is worth that. Beautiful isn't it? They say she washed in nothing but milk."

"She lost her head. Two hundred and fifty."

"Five hundred thousand, papa. If I don't come back you make a profit of two hundred thousand."

The old man looked at Paul's evening dress. "You go to the Casino, perhaps? Then you won't come back.

Three hundred thousand at ten per cent interest a day. You know it is illegal for me to do this?"

"We all have our worries, papa. The pawn-shop is shut and I need the money tonight. The little Buddha is exquisite. It should be in the Louvre. Three hundred and fifty thousand and seven per cent a day."

"Maybe the little Buddha does come from the Louvre? You have, perhaps, the Mona Lisa as well?"

"Next week, papa."

The man's chin came off his chest and a pair of watery brown eyes stared at Paul. Then he smiled and began to collect the objects together. "Three hundred and twenty-five thousand at—"

"Seven per cent."

The old man shrugged his shoulders and got the money from his till.

Paul picked up the notes and then he counted out ten thousand five hundred francs and passed them back.

"What is this for, monsieur?"

"The ring that belongs to Mademoiselle Elise Benoit, papa."

"Eleven thousand, monsieur."

Paul shook his head sadly, "Papa, were you never in love? Does a woman's distress mean nothing to you?"

The old man smiled. "Yes, and yes, my son. But now I am sixty and in business. It is you who are in love … Is that a time to be mean and to argue over five hundred francs?"

Paul passed over another five hundred francs and the ring was handed to him in a little box. As Paul left the shop the jeweller called after him:

"She has a temper at times, my son. But do not be alarmed. It is the salt that brings out the true savour of love ... Bonne chance!"

Outside Paul dismissed his chauffeur and walked along to the *Dauphin Vert*.

Elise was sitting in a little alcove with a glass of white wine and a plate of *moules marinières*. Paul walked up to her and with a smile took the other seat at the table.

"*Bonsoir, Mademoiselle Benoit*," he said.

"*Bonsoir, monsieur je-ne-sais-qui*, and I would like to point out that there are plenty of other tables unoccupied at which you might sit."

"Ashcroft is the name, Paul Ashcroft. I have often said that only a French woman knows how to eat shell-fish with grace and elegance, and you, mademoiselle, are all grace and elegance."

"For an Englishman you speak French too well."

"My mother was French."

She was watching him closely, her face a little grave but with the hint of amusement somewhere in her eyes.

"Then your mother should have instructed you that a gentleman does not sit uninvited at a lady's table."

"My mother was very absent-minded, mademoiselle. She must have forgotten."

"You wish to talk to me?"

"If you like. But I am quite happy just to watch you."

Paul looked at her and he could have gone on looking for hours. It was odd really. He had seen girls as beautiful before, and had fallen in love with them. But not with quite such a bump and a boost to the blood circulation. The way she fished a mussel from its shell and carried it to that lovely mouth was sheer poetry … the way her arms moved … he sighed.

"It would be better, monsieur, perhaps if you talked. When you just look you have a silly expression on your face." She smiled fleetingly.

"Mademoiselle, I am in love with you."

She nodded gravely and then ate two more mussels, took a sip of wine and finally said, "So?"

"That is all. I am in love with you."

She looked at him shrewdly for a moment and then, cocking one eyebrow in a movement that entranced Paul, said: "You are certain that your father was an Englishman and not a Spaniard?"

Paul nodded. "Ashcroft. James Wigmore Ashcroft, the biggest boot manufacturer in the Midlands of England. The firm was started during the Crimean War … supplying boots to the army."

"Ah, I understand. It happens during every war. Profiteering. So, your father makes boots. What do you make?"

"I spend the money he makes making boots. And I am in love with you."

"So, now we have had your biography. At least it has the merit of being short—if dull. Or maybe you wish to sell me some boots?"

"I wish just to be with you."

"You are a young man who usually gets what he wants?"

"But of course."

"It is good then that for once you should be disappointed. Raoul!" She raised her voice a little and called to the waiter.

"You wish for something else?" said Paul eagerly. "Please let me order it…"

"It is not necessary, monsieur. I can order for myself." Raoul came to the table. He was big, blue-jowled and muscularly amiable.

"Mademoiselle Elise?" The way he spoke showed that for her he would do anything. Paul knew just how he felt.

"Raoul—tell this gentleman that if he has not left the place within ten seconds you will be obliged to throw him out."

Raoul grinned. "*Avec plaisir … c'est un de ces types, eh? Monsieur …?*" he turned to Paul.

Paul rose.

"I'm going. But the wonderful fact remains that I love you."

Raoul answered for her.

"It is not a wonder, monsieur. The whole town loves mademoiselle. You are one among many. *Et puis, alors, vat'en!*"

He advanced on Paul who backed away with good grace, gave Elise a little bow and then made for the door. But behind him on the table, to be discovered by her later, Paul left the little box with the ring in it.

Half-an-hour later Paul, elated with love, was at the Casino shrewdly looking round the over-rich crowd in search of his first victim. Paul never gambled at the Casinos, there was little excitement in it for him, and he knew better ways of gaining and getting rid of money.

Within ten minutes his mind was made up. He picked a Signora Busoni—he obtained those facts later—the middleaged widow of a Milan industrialist (silk, motor-scooters and a patent cream for developing the bust), wearing a magenta dress, plump, a little giggly, and with a thick hoar frost of diamonds about her neck and wrists.

He watched her play for a while, then followed her into the bar, and in no time at all was sharing a bottle of champagne with her.

He drank, toasting, "La bella Italia ..." and then, lowering his glass, an appealing melancholy in his eyes, he blinked as her diamonds glittered like chips of blue ice. Before he left her their friendship was well under way.

Within a week Paul was firmly established at the villa. He engaged a cook and a couple of maids to help Madame Fouret, and he now began to entertain. Chiefly Signora Busoni. And through Signora Busoni he was introduced to other wealthy people in the district. Monsieur Paul became a great favourite ... always smiling, always so gay, always ready to throw himself into the spirit of a party ... Madame Fouret quite took him to heart. She was never neglected. He gave her little presents and was full of compliments for the way she ran the house for him. And for her it was a pleasure to have the villa alive with people ... to have around her always the stir of a happy, changing company. Comte d'Auxier had seldom done any entertaining.

Half-way through the second week Paul decided that he must start work. His money was running out.

On an evening when he was due to call for Signora Busoni and take her to a party, he telephoned her.

"Signora ... I have to drive to Cannes on urgent business this evening. I am heartbroken. But I will be back as soon as I can and join you at the party ... Yes, very urgent business, *cara signora*. It would have to be to tear me away from such a charming companion..."

He heard her rich giggle at the other end of the line.

He waited an hour and then went and took his car out without the chauffeur. He drove along the coast, through the town and parked his car about half a mile beyond Signora Busoni's villa which faced the sea.

He knew the villa well from his visits there, and he knew, too, that the old couple who looked after it for Signora Busoni always spent their evenings in the kitchen playing cards and arguing with one another.

Whistling gently to himself he walked back along the road to the villa, keeping in the shadows. Ten minutes later he was in the villa garden, but not whistling now. He could see a light in the back of the villa where the old couple sat in the kitchen. He pulled on a pair of black gloves and a few moments later was climbing up one of the pillars of the balcony that fronted Signora Busoni's bedroom. He went in through the french windows and, once inside, pulled the heavy curtains and switched on the light. He crossed to the door and locked it on the inside.

It was a small room, floridly decorated and the air heavy with perfume. He stood with a reflective smile on his face. The trouble with wealthy widows like Signora Busoni, apart from not willingly sharing their good fortune with others, was that they talked too much. Already he knew where the safe was; behind a small picture near the bed. He took the picture down and eyed the safe quizzically. It had a combination lock. Paul from long experience knew that it might take him anything from five minutes to three hours to listen to the fall of the tumblers and break the combination. Women hated such locks. They were always afraid of forgetting the combination. It took him fifteen minutes to find

Where Signora Busoni had written the combination. It was in a little telephone number book in a drawer of an escritoire near the window. She'd listed it as 'Busoni 7835' which Paul knew was not the telephone number of her villa. Originally a clever idea, mused Paul, as he worked the lock, but like all good ideas it had suffered from popularity and publicity.

He opened the safe door and within five minutes the contents of the jewel cases were deposited in the bottom of a silk pillow case that he took from the bed. He went round the room and skimmed the cream of its contents, putting them one by one in the case, the silver dressing table fittings, a gold wristlet watch and, surprisingly, a photograph of Signora Busoni in a plain leather frame. Then, after unlocking the bedroom door, Paul drew the curtains and left. It was all done quietly and calmly. A young man in evening dress and black gloves occupying himself soberly with his professional business … a young man who knew that the world was his oyster and had no intention of letting the knife slip and cut him as he opened it.

Signora Busoni was delighted when Paul arrived at the party just before midnight. She was delighted when he danced with her and delighted when he offered to drive her home. She would not have been delighted had she known what was locked away in the boot of the car.

He went in with her for a drink before he left for his own villa.

"Fix yourself a drink, *caro* Paul, while I go up and get rid of this wrap and freshen my face …"

"Can I mix one for you?"

"No thank you."

As she disappeared up the stairs Paul poured himself a large brandy and also one for her. He knew she would need it when she came down. He knew so well how the scene would go—and quite frankly it was the one moment in the whole process which he did not like. Taking money from the rich caused him no qualms; but the sight of distress on any woman's face disturbed him … However, it never lasted long.

The whole scene went exactly as he knew it would. Signora Busoni appeared at the head of the stairs, a large, plumpish figure in a purple evening gown, a thick rope of pearls about her neck, and throwing her arms high cried, "Paul … Oh, Paul … ! The most terrible thing! I've been robbed…" And then she was bouncing down the stairs as fast as she could, crying, "The police! The police!"

Paul stopped her at the bottom of the stairs with a glass of brandy. He helped her to a chair and fussed around her. "Drink your brandy, dear signora … It is the best thing for shock. What a dreadful affair … and while you were dancing so happily … There, there, don't move I shall arrange everything." He filled her glass again, and then said, "May I go up and have a look? I have some experience in these matters ..."

"Oh, Paul, you are so kind ... such a comfort at a moment like this ..."

"Sit there, dear signora ... and leave everything to me."

Paul disappeared upstairs and was soon down again. He stood in front of Signora Busoni, his face solemn and thoughtful.

"What is it, Paul?" she asked.

"You know exactly what has been taken?"

"But of course. I have only to look to tell ..." And Signora Busoni rattled off a list of missing effects which omitted nothing as Paul well knew. She finished up, "Even a photograph of myself the thief took."

Paul looked speculatively at her. "Really? A photograph..." He was silent, his brows puckered in thought.

"Why do you look like that, Paul?"

He reached out and put a hand on her shoulder comfortingly. "It was just a thought ... Still, there might be something in it ..." Then with a shake of his head, he said, "No, there couldn't be. Our best plan is to inform the police." As he moved towards the telephone he said half to himself, "But it's odd ... very odd. I wonder ...?"

"Paul—what's in your mind? Tell me. Why should a thief take a valueless photograph?"

He turned back to her, nursing his glass of brandy. "Signora Busoni," he said gravely, "I think, maybe, I can answer that question. I think, maybe. I see some hope—"

"You do?" she cried expectantly. "Oh, Paul—tell me."

He took her hand and stroked it sympathetically.

"You must be patient with me. You see, some years ago while I was staying in Marseille I did a service for a man who is known as Gringo the Greek. He is ... well, a big man in the underworld there. A thief but an unusual one. I do not wish to go into the details of the help I gave him. except that it was quite legitimate and he was very grateful."

"You think he stole my jewels?"

"I am certain, dear signora. You see, I became very friendly with him and once he took me to his house and showed me an extraordinary thing. All around his room there were photographs of men and women. It is a kind of kink with him that whenever he does a job he takes a photograph of the person he has robbed..."

"What a monster!"

"In some ways, yes. But in others, no. He is a man who has a good side to him."

"For that I care nothing, Paul," said Signora Busoni sharply. "We must telephone the police about him at once."

"But of course." He moved towards the telephone. Then he stopped and turned towards her, his eyes full of friendly concern. "But would it help? He will have alibis ... and you may never see your jewels again. But because you are my friend, dear signora, and I would do anything for you, I could go to him. He will do anything for me."

"You mean that he would give you my things back?" There was a rising note of hope in her voice.

"Well not quite ... But he might sell them back?"

"But why should I pay for my own jewels!" Hope was now replaced by outrage.

Paul nodded. "Of course it's outrageous, dear signora ..." He filled her brandy glass for her again. "But look at it like this. If we call in the police, isn't there a great risk you won't get your jewels back? Gringo's very clever, and very slippery ..." He paused, sipping his brandy. "But he's a man who always remembers his friends. If I could talk to him." He saw that she was hanging on his word now. This was the moment, the fraction of time when a woman swings between two minds. "What are the jewels worth?" he asked.

"Ten million francs at least."

"So, ten thousand pounds. To return them and make a little profit for himself and to oblige me because you are my dear friend ... he might charge, say, a thousand pounds ... a million francs ... No, no ..." Paul turned away from her. "Perhaps the whole idea is stupid. Why should he do this for me? Maybe we should tell the police."

Signora Busoni considered this. Then her mind like a calculating machine produced its answer.

"Paul," her voice was suddenly solemn behind him. He turned.

"Paul, it would be worth trying—if you think you might get them back for that price?"

"I shall do everything ... everything. But if it succeeds, signora, then no one must ever know. Our secret, *cara signora*. If the police knew we might both be in trouble."

"Paul ... you must do this. Offer a million francs—but not a sou more!"

"Dear lady." Paul took her hand and kissed it. "Tomorrow I go to Marseille. I shall do my best, of course."

Paul did do his best. Two days later Signora Busoni got her jewels back—for a million and a half francs. The money was paid in cash to Paul to be handed to Gringo. So far as Paul knew Gringo might no longer be alive. Long, long ago he had vaguely known a small crook of that name in Marseille and more than once he had used his name on occasions like this. The cash went into a large, old-fashioned safe in the billiard room at the Villa Triton to which Madame Fouret had given Paul the key.

The following morning Paul was sunbathing on the villa's bathing stage when Madame Fouret brought a visitor down to him.

"Mademoiselle Benoit," she announced. She withdrew towards the villa, her back stiff and disapproving.

Paul stood up and the blood rushing to his head made the world turn over giddily before his eyes, a swirl of blue sky, pink villa and dark cypress trees and at the centre of the cartwheel a slim, cool figure in a white silk dress, a touch of scarlet scarf at the throat to match the soft scarlet lips. The wheel steadied and Elise was smiling at him.

"Monsieur, it has taken me a little while to find you."

"Call me Paul, please."

She hesitated for a moment, raised an eyebrow doubtfully and deliciously and then with a little laugh suddenly said, "All right ... Paul."

"Ha ... thank you, Elise. Now the morning is perfect."

"I came to thank you for returning my ring. It was very generous of you. But I cannot accept it without—"

Paul frowned and stepped forward menacingly. "Elise, if you are now going to try and pay me back I shall pick you up and throw you into the sea. Can you swim?"

"Yes."

"A pity. Because I could then have jumped in and saved you. However, let us have no talk of money. I have more than I know what to do with."

"I was not going to offer, you money. In the first place it would be ungracious to spoil a generous act and, secondly, I could not afford it. But in return I should like you to accept this ..."

From behind her back she produced a little bronze figure of Hermes.

"... it was brought up by a fisherman—"

"I know," said Paul. "It's beautiful. But this fisherman of ours doesn't he ever catch fish?"

Elise laughed, and to Paul the sound was like a little burst of the most exquisite music on the hot morning air. "Between ourselves, Monsieur Paul—"

"Paul."

"Paul. I make them in my studio. But they are none the less good for that," she said stoutly.

"Of course not. But isn't it a little dishonest to tell this story—"

"About the fisherman? Why? All the world is just a little dishonest. If I sell one to an American for thirty dollars it really is worth that ... and it pleases them to have a little story attached to it. Also, they think they have got a bargain ... a Roman antique for thirty dollars! They go away thinking I am naive and have no sense of money."

Paul smiled. "You make other fa—I mean antiques?"

"A few. I can turn out anything from an unmistakeable Picasso to an authentic Etruscan vase."

"You're wonderful."

"I am very good."

"And I love you, Elise."

"Monsieur, you should not say that lightly to any woman."

"I do not say it lightly or to any woman. I say it to you and I mean it."

"And after it is said, what then?"

"It is out of my hands. It is up to the woman to advance or retreat, to say yes or no."

"You are a curious one. When you smile I do not believe what you say. But when you frown and have that sad look in your eyes, then I think maybe there is a real person somewhere."

"You will have dinner with me tonight? At the *Dauphin Vert*?"

"I regret—"

"At eight o'clock."

"Impossible."

"And I shall take you for a drive afterwards."

"You are ridiculous."

"But good company."

"You should go into your father's business instead of squandering his money. You would be good at selling boots. Au revoir ... Paul. Eight o'clock."

After she had gone Paul sat in a quiet trance until lunchtime.

Some men hurry home from work to their wives and family. But more men hurry back to pursue some passion, like fretwork, pigeon-keeping, philately ... square-dancing, bowls, darts ... something from which there is no escape. Victims of their own natures they live in happy bondage. Paul was a victim … not of philately, but of philanthropy. He couldn't help it. His education had been all wrong; too much Robin Hood and not enough Adam Smith; his head was full of romance and a dishonest life had turned the milk of human kindness in him to a rich, full cream. He held the selfish view that the best thing to be done with money was to spend it on other people. It was a vice with him.

And now, being in love, the urge to throw money away was ten times as strong. He was in love and he wanted the world to be as happy as he was. After lunch he went into action. Even without Elise it would have happened. But now Paul was full of an even greater contempt for accepted economics. While Madame Fouret was safely having her siesta, Paul got his case with the Monsieur Durobat clothes and make-up and went down into the cellar under the villa. In the cellar he changed into the guise of Monsieur Durobat, whistling contentedly to himself, and then made his way from the cellar through a narrow tunnel he had discovered that led to a small grotto in the garden.

An hour later he was in the town and things began to happen. A young typist in the bus office was surprised when a bearded, dignified old man with the button of the Legion of Honour walked in, raised his hat, presented her with a large bottle of Channel No. 5 and was gone before she could say a word. A woman at a stall in the market was surprised to find a ten thousand franc note under her weights just after an old gentleman had bought some oranges from her. The oranges were given to a small boy who found in the bag with them a mouth organ.

In the early days of his new economic system Paul had found it hard to get rid of money. Most people, he know, resented direct charity. The natural dignity and self-respect in people made them capable of facing their own problems. But there wasn't a person in the world who could resist a surprise, an extravagant, anonymous gift from heaven. Such a one was Madame Fouret's sister, who that afternoon was visited by Monsieur Durobat who insisted that the vase he had seen on the window table in her little house was Sèvres and just the piece he had been looking for. He paid fifty thousand francs for it and walked off leaving her with the feeling that the world was crazy and delightful and the prospect of Aix-les-Bains now assured. The vase Paul dropped into the sea. Nowadays he was so practised that he could have cleared a million francs in a couple of hours easily.

Monsieur Durobat finished up the afternoon sitting on a seat in the garden of an orphanage run by the Convent of the Sacred Heart. All around him the children were at play. He had a decided weakness for children. While he was sitting there Sister Thérèse who was in charge of the children came and sat by him in the shade and very soon they were chatting to one another. Sister Therese was a wrinkled old apple of a woman who looked as though she would keep for ever. She had a heart of gold, a mind as keen as a new razor blade, and one conviction—that God and children and good drains were the most important things in life. After a few moments she wrote Monsieur Durobat down as wealthy, sentimental and lonely, and she knew these were the qualities from which large subscriptions came. Privately she asked God in advance to forgive her for her worldly cupidity, and then went to work. She found it unexpectedly easy. When Monsieur Durobat rose to go he pulled out his wallet and handed her fifty thousand francs.

"Sister, you will do me a kindness if you take this for the children."

"Monsieur is very generous."

"Not at all. It is easy to make money if you have the talent. But hard to spend it wisely. Spend it frivolously, sister. Buy the girls pink hair-ribbons and the boys ... well, you will know."

"Monsieur is very understanding. Some other time it will be a pleasure to show you round the orphanage. The bathrooms ... they will disgust you. For years we have dreamed of raising enough money to build a new wing. And the kitchen, monsieur ... so difficult to keep clean, so unhygienic and old-fashioned. Yes, yes, you must see it all the next time you come."

Moniseur Durobat left the town unobtrusively and picked up his bicycle from a little wood on the outskirts.

At the other end of his journey he hid the bicycle in the pine wood by the cove, and then went into the villa through the cellar.

Later that evening he motored into town to meet Elise. He spent three wonderful hours with her. Although she still did not take him seriously, she showed that she liked him and after dinner they sat for an hour in the car on the coast road, watching the moon come up over the sea. It was the biggest, yellowest moon Paul had ever seen and he sat blissfully holding Elise's hand. He didn't try to kiss her. He was content just to be with her.

When he left her at her studio just before midnight he did not go home. He went to the casino and found Signora Busoni there with some friends. He might be in love and not know what to do about it. But he was also in business and he more than knew what to do about that. That night he marked down a Madame Lepâtre, the wife of a Bordeaux wine merchant.

And so the days went on. Love and business. Paul saw Elise as much as he could and now knew a lot about her. She lived with her young brother who was an artist of great promise. But the two were very poor and it was Elise's ambition to save enough money for them to go to Paris where her brother could study.

Monsieur Durobat was now known in the town, a mysterious figure who came and went, leaving cash surprises behind him. Meanwhile Paul Ashcroft worked. The cash in the safe mounted up and each transaction was carefully noted on a slip of paper also locked away with the money.

After a month the slip of paper made interesting reading.

Busoni	1,500,000 francs.
Lepâtre	2,000,000 do.
Sturgess	2,500,000 do.
Bloire	500,000 do.
Brunot	1,000,000 do.

Mrs. Sturgess was an American holidaying in Europe without her husband and regarded the whole thing as a high adventure. Paul had the greatest difficulty in persuading her that she could not accompany him to interview Gringo. Bloire was a disappointment. She was Swiss, stubborn and tight-fisted. It took Paul two and a half hours to work the combination on her safe and then he found that half the jewellery was paste. Only twice did Paul fail. One safe he had been unable to open and while working on the other had been disturbed. But on the whole he was a happy young man and he looked after his flock well, those who had been fleeced and those waiting to be fleeced. He still took Signora

Busoni dancing, still invited Mesdames Lepâtre, Bloire and Brunot to his villa and took a genuine pleasure in their company. That they had too much money and he felt obliged to spend it wisely for them didn't for one moment prejudice him against them. When Mrs. Sturgess, away on her travels by now, arrived in Rome and then Athens she found flowers from him waiting in her hotel room.

But you can't mix love and business. Paul should have known this. But like most men he had to learn it the hard way. He came back one afternoon after playing the part of Monsieur Durobat, edged through the bushes to the grotto in the garden and then slipped in and along the tunnel to the cellar. By the light of a single candle perched on top of a bin of Montrachet '24 he stripped off his make-up and began to change back into his own clothes. He was whistling happily but a little off key to himself. Life was good. More money had piled up in the old safe and Monsieur Durobat was having the time of his life getting rid of it. He pulled on his trousers and was about to knot a tie round his neck when a voice from a shadowed archway behind him said:

"There was an occasion when I said your biography was short and dull. I take it back."

Paul turned round very slowly. He knew the voice and he knew what to expect. He found himself facing Elise.

His heart went bump, but this time the noise was like a sack of wet flour hitting a muddy floor.

"Elise," he said, gulping, "you shouldn't be here."

"But naturally, *mon ami*." She was smiling but there was no comfort in the smile. "Well ..." One little toe was tapping on the stone slab of the floor.

"Well, what?"

"Explain, *mon petit chou* ... You know in France there is a very long prison sentence for pretending to be a Chevalier of the Legion of Honour."

Paul gave another gulp and found some of his confidence.

"There is no law which says a man can't give money away. Do good by stealth ... it's a proverb."

"Ah, a proverb ... very interesting ... Tell me more. You give away your father's money? You like to do good?"

"Naturally ... and how the devil did you find out?"

"How did I find out? *Mon ami*, you need your head examined. I make fakes. I recognize there when I see them. False beards and moustaches—Pouff! An old man with a young man's eyes—Pouff! For other people it is all right. Not for me. But what is the game? For more than three weeks now the town talks about this curious Monsieur Durobat ... so good, so kind, so eccentric, so wealthy. Thousands of francs drop from heaven on people's heads—"

"That's better than rain."

"You think? Maybe not for some people." She threw a roll of franc notes on the floor before him. "Not for me. Not for my brother. Oh, yes, I tell you one evening that I am poor because I save everything to send my brother, who one day will be a great artist, to Paris ... And what happens?"

"Well, he will be a great artist. I saw some of his stuff. It's good. Better than yours. And anyway don't throw money around like that." Paul bent and picked up the roll of notes.

"Bah!" She stamped her foot. "So, this kind Monsieur Durobat comes along a few days later and buys two of my brother's worst canvases for an incredible sum ... enough to send him to Paris."

"Well, he wants to go to Paris, doesn't he?"

"But not this way."

"What's wrong with this way?"

"Ah—it is for that that I wish your answer. What is wrong, eh? You think I have nothing in here but wool?" She tapped her head with one finger vigorously and at the same time bore down on him. "Explain, you little half-English half-French pig!"

"Now, now, Elise ... calm down. It's my money. I can do, what I like with it. And you shouldn't have followed me, spied on me ... Why, it's ... it's not right."

But Elise was not to be put off, she grabbed him by the ears and, her face a few inches from his, looked him straight in the eyes. "Tell me, *cochon*—is it your money to give away or not?"

"But Elise—"

"Tell me!" For a second or two his head was shaken vigorously and her face danced before his eyes. "Your money or not?"

"Well ..."

"The truth ... and remember the jeweller in town is a friend of mine and we chat often. I find it difficult to understand why a rich English monsieur should need to pawn things belonging to his friend the Count of Auxier."

"But they're out of pawn now. Back in the house."

"So it is not your money!"

For a moment there was silence between them. When she was angry, Paul was thinking, she looked lovelier than ever and there was a quality about her that filled him with inexpressible longing. He sighed ...

"No, Elise. It isn't my money. I can't lie to you—"

"You would if you could. *Bon!* Now sit down and tell me all about it." She pushed him, making him sit down on a case of *Pol Roger, Cuvée de Reserve, 1943*, and stood threateningly over him. She needed only a tricolour hat, and a scythe blade on a pole to look like the spirit of the French revolution. Paul, loved her more than ever, and wondered whether to tell her the truth or invent some fiction that might not entirely blacken him. He told her the truth—much to his surprise. This was love.

She listened to him without interruption except for occasional and obscure monosyllabic French expressions of angry surprise and when he had finished she said forcibly:

"It is shameful ... to make love to silly old women and then steal their money!"

"I don't make love to them."

"Who is to know that?"

"And anyway they don't miss their money and I do a lot of good with it. And anyway again, I don't see what you have to bellyache about—"

"Don't use such terms to me, *cochon*!"

"Why complain, then? Why should you complain? You're just as dishonest with your fake antiques ..." He grinned, and in a high falsetto said, "one of the fishermen. dragged it up in his net..."

"It's such a little thing—"

"Doesn't matter."

"And the American had too much money

"No excuse. Dishonesty is dishonesty ... small or big. It's the principle that counts, Elise."

"Don't lecture me." She was silent for a moment and one wonderful eyebrow went up cocked in thought, Then she asked, "How much money have you got left in that safe?"

"I don't know. About six million francs."

"Then you must get rid of it. At once."

"I must?"

"Yes. Give it to sister Thérèse. You can't give it back to the people you took it from.. It'll be just enough to build the new bathrooms and the kitchens—"

"You know about that?"

Elise rolled her eyes at his naivety. "The whole town knows. Sister Thérèse talks of nothing else but the clever way she is handling this mysterious Monsieur Durobat. In the *Dauphin Vert* they are laying bets that she will get the money before the month is out. She will, too. Tomorrow."

"If you say so," said Paul meekly. "And then how soon after that will you be ready to leave?"

"Leave?" Elise's eyes widened, dark and puzzled.

"But of course. That's what you mean, isn't it? Oh, Elise, you make me very happy." Paul. stood up and took her hand. "I've been. waiting for this moment so long. We'll go to Paris ... and later we'll send for your brother."

Elise stepped back from him. "I don't know what you're talking about."

"But of course you do. It's obvious." Paul put out his hands and took her shoulders lovingly. "You get angry because you think I make love to these old women. You take the trouble to find out all about me and when you know the truth ... what do you do? Go to me police like a good citizen? No, you come to ms. You couldn't say more clearly that you love me. Darling," he bent forward and kissed her on the cheek. "Do we got married here or in Paris?"

"You're crazy!" Her voice made a faint echo in the cobwebbed arches.

"I know, with love."

"But I don't—"

"But you do."

Paul put his arms round her and drew her to him. She came like a hypnotised bird. Then his lips were on hers and there was a roll of sound in his ears as though he had a hundred drums beating instead of a single heart. And suddenly the bird was no longer hypnotised and there was warmth and movement in the soft lips under his own.

Suddenly, she drew away from him, gave a little gasp and then, her face radiant whispered huskily, "*Ma foi* … it is true. I am crazy. I am in love…" And then reaching for him moving swiftly into his arms, she sighed, "Now let us do it again… Now that I know what it is all about and can give my mind to it…"

"*Cheri*…" Sigh.

"*Cherie*…" Sigh, cut short.

And then much later, sitting side by side on a case of champagne, Elise said with a sigh of content:

"In Paris we shall be so happy."

"Of course. We will open an an antique shop. Your fakes will go well, and I should meet many rich people—"

"No, nothing like that. We will work hard—and honestly."

"You mean that?" Surprise filled Paul's voice. "Not even an occasional—"

"No." And it was the 'No' of a woman shaping a man's future.

"But why? Hard work is so dull."

"It is respectable. What child could respect a parent who was not honest?"

"What child is this?"

"Our children. They must be proud of their papa and mamma—"

"Children!" Paul's voice echoed weakly around the cellar.

"Yes. Five. Three boys and two girls. I have it all planned. An honest, respectable family. That is marriage. You agree?" There was loving threat in the last two words.

Paul sighed. "I agree."

Elise smiled contentedly and put her arms round his neck.

"*Cheri*—I am glad you insist."

"*Cherie* …"

And so it was arranged later, over a bottle of Pommery, taken on the terrace with the sea like mauve velvet and the sky full of polished stars and a swollen moon, that the next morning Paul should give the money to Sister Thérèse and that a new life should start for them both. It would be hard at first they both knew, for dishonesty, small or big, is a habit hard to break.

But they were young and they were in love, two things which add up to optimism; and what is there that can stand against optimism? They sat, hand in hand on the terrace, undisturbed because Madame Fouret had gone into town to visit her sister. The next morning while Paul was having his breakfast Madame Fouret came to him and, after a certain amount of skirmishing, said, "Monsieur ... my sister goes to Aix-les-Bains today and I was wondering ..."

Paul nodded. "But, of course. You must go with her on the journey to look after her, and also perhaps you should stay a few days to see her settled in?"

"Ah, monsieur, you are so understanding and so kind ..."

"Not at all, Madame Fouret. Tell the chauffeur to run you into town as soon as you are ready."

And when she came back from Aix-les-Bains thought Paul, he would be gone. But he would leave a present for her. It was the best way to say goodbye.

Madame Fouret left about ten o'clock. Paul had a swim and then before changing he went to the old safe which was in one corner of the villa's billiard room and opened it.

There was just over six million francs in it ... six thousand pounds ... Six million would be a fine present for Sister Thérèse and the surplus would allow him to tip his servants, buy a few presents and still have enough to take him to Paris. Elise, he felt, would understand that a man was entitled to dishonest travelling expenses when he journeyed to an honest living. He locked the money back in the safe and put the key in the pocket of his bath robe. This afternoon he would change into his Monsieur Durobat disguise and go to see Sister Thérèse. It was going to be a red letter day for her.

As a matter of fact, it was going to be quite a day for Paul, though he was blissfully unaware of it as he picked up a cue and began to knock a ball about the billiard table.

He was just about to play a difficult cannon shot and screw his own ball back off the top cushion into the bottom left-hand pocket when a shadow fell across the table.

Paul looked up. The billiard room had a long run of wide windows facing out over the garden with a glimpse of the sea showing between two acacia trees, and in the centre of the windows was an open doorway. Standing just inside the doorway was a curious trio.

In front, leaning forward with his large, fat, beringed hands resting on the top of a gold-headed cane was a man with the stature and heavy-fowled face of a Napoleon. He yore a dove-grey suit, a black stock with a pearl-headed pin, lilac spats and a flat crowned felt hat with the brim turned up. The hat was tipped forward, giving the impression that it rested on his eyebrows which were strong and bushy. There was a certain vow-like amiability about the large face which was strengthened by a gentle cud-chewing action of his mouth.

On his right was a tall, solemn-faced individual in a tight navy-blue suit, the jacket open to shown an even tighter blue-and-white horizontally striped fisherman's vest. He wore a white cloth cap and a frown, both of them the worse for wear. The other person on the left was a youth of about seventeen with a pink-and-white handsome face, a vacant smile, brown eyes full of wonder, and an open mouth. He wore an open leather jerkin with a mermaid painted on each arm, a blue silk shirt, red canvas trousers and white shoes.

"Monsieur Ashcroft?" enquired the man in the dovegrey suit and his voice was as rich as bouillabaisse.

"Yes." Paul put his cue down. "Who are you and what do you want?"

The man smiled and there was a flash of three gold teeth. He handed his cane to the youth and then picked up the cue Paul had just put down. He leaned over the table and, as he prepared for a shot, he said, "A good question and well put. Shows a keen, direct mind … I like it. One must be a bit of a psychologist these days to succeed. Must be able to mark a man down at once … particularly in business. Yes …" He played the shot and the ball screwed back off the cushion into the bottom pocket. "Sweet," he sighed and straightened up.

"I think," said Paul cautiously, "you'd better explain yourself a little more clearly."

"Naturally ... but it takes time. The use of words is involved. Oh, yes ... and psychology. Must assess a man before you know which screw to put on him." He set the balls up for another shot.

"Interesting," said Paul. "Put if you don't mind, I'll call the gardener and chauffeur and have you thrown out."

"Counter measure. Violence. But ineffective. I'll explain why later, but I'm glad you brought it up because it's good for the boy ... experience." He tipped his head over his shoulder towards the youth in the jerkin and said, "My articled pupil. Not good material but in time we'll make something out of him. Close your mouth, André," he said gently and then played his shot.

"I could., of course, telephone for the police," said Paul.

"You could ..." The gold teeth. flashed again and the rings of one hand winked as he chalked the top of the cue.

"Unwise," said the tall thin man in the navy-blue suit, and his voice had the resonance of a slide of wet gravel.

"My secretary," said the man in the dove-grey suit proudly. "Accounts and legal department. Monsieur Plume ... but no dress sense." He bent forward, cocked his head as he looked along the line of his shot and said vaguely, "It's a big old-fashioned safe. How much have you got in it?"

"Look, what the hell do you. think—" Paul made a hasty forward movement but he stopped abruptly.

Monsieur Plume and André were staring down at their right hands and the surprise on their faces matched that on Paul's. Each hand held a revolver.

"Sweet," said the man in the dove-grey suit. "But André, hold it a little higher and remember what I told you. You must have the safety catch off … That's better." He turned his head back and played his shot, potting the red with a neat, brisk stroke. "How much in the safe?" he asked straightening up.

Paul, although no sailor, had enough sense not to row against tide and wind.

"Nothing," he said, setting an oblique course.

"Try again."

And somehow Monsieur Plume and Andre had moved forward and were crowding Paul a little, and André's vacant grin had become a dog-like pant.

"Just over six million francs," Paul confessed. "And in my opinion the explanations are taking far too long."

"The preliminaries," said Monsieur Dove-Grey, "must be observed. Opportunity for studying character on both sides." He moved away from the table and sinking into a large wicker chair, carefully adjusted the crease of his trousers and then took a cigar from a case. André stretched out his left hand and held a lighter for him.

"Thank you, Andre. And now, Monsieur Ashcroft, the key please."

"I haven't got the key. I've lost it. I've thrown it into the sea, It's with my lawyers. Take your choice. And anyway it's not my money."

"Good, good," said the man amiably. "You notice that, André? Bluster, smoke-screen ... but not from nervousness or fear. Gives him time to think; time to plan. Well, André, you know the answer to that. Cut right through it. After all we know where the key is, don't we. Remember we were looking through the window a little while ago ..."

As he spoke Monsieur Plume and André, eager and swift, closed in on Paul. A revolver dug him in the back and another in the stomach. He coughed at the concerted pressures and Andre's hand relieved him of the key in the pocket of his beach robe.

"Sweet," said their master. "Sweet ... End of preliminaries. Now to business. No, no, André—" he said sharply as the youth made a move towards the safe. "Not that at all. That's crude, unprofessional and, above all, unethical." Then, from behind a dove-grey cloud of cigar smoke, he said benignly to Paul, "I'm surprised, monsieur, that you don't know me. We did meet many, many years ago—and since then—though. I take no offence—you have gone on exaggerating our acquaintance." He stood up and gave a plump little bow. "I am Kyro Chrysantos—"

"As far as I'm concerned you can be Father Christmas!" said Paul angrily.

"No, no … you don't understand yet. Kyro Chrysantos. Or to you, monsieur, Gringo the Greek … Ha, you look surprised." Paul was surprised. He sat down suddenly in the chair behind him. As he did so a change came over the company. The air of enigma and threat went and an easy sense of camaraderie blossomed. Monsieur Plume gave Paul a cigarette and André lit it for him and Monsieur Chrysantos said with a gentle wave of his cigar, "It. is a nice place you have appropriated here and believe me, monsieur, I am full of admiration for you. You do us all credit. Ah, André, if I could only hope that one day you would be as successful as monsieur here…"

"Tell me," said Paul, recovering and by no means resigned to drifting for long helpless before. wind and tide, "how did you learn about me? I thought you were dead or on Devil's Island."

"Both those pleasures, monsieur Paul, are happily remote. Notice now, André, this is the period of consolidation… the *va-et-vient* of cross talk before moving into the last stage which is, of course, amicable settlement—"

"Look," said Paul, "couldn't you cut out the lectures? Let him do it by correspondence course or something. How did you find out?"

"But he is young, monsieur. You and I were young once and we had to learn. Besides his father has paid me a large premium. This is a morning André will never forget."

"Or me," said Paul.

"Or me," said Monsieur Plume.

"Or me," said Chrysantos. "So, we are all happy. Yes, monsieur Paul … we are happy. And now I tell you. Sometime ago a lady, an American lady called Sturgess, is spending a few days, in Marseille and in every bar she is asking for Gringo the Greek. She wants to see him. And this comes to my ears so I oblige her …"

"Oh, lord!"

"It is all right, monsieur. I listened to her and I did not give you away. It seems that I stole her jewels and you bought them back from me. It is good. I take her on a tour of the underworld. She is fun. I make a little money from her. I give her my autograph and she goes away happy. And after that I decide to come here and find Monsieur Ashcroft. For two weeks now, monsieur, we have been in the town watching you. And now we are here, and the partnership is complete. But six million francs is not much. I should have thought you would have had more than that."

"I have had heavy expenses and I'm an extravagant spender."

"Who is not? But to split this among four … it is very little. Five million between you and me and half a million each for my friends … No, it is not enough."

"Oh, you mean to let me keep some? That's very generous."

"But of course. You have made it—by using my name. So we share. But it is too little considering your talent and the value of my name. Notice, André, that little money is for little men. Big money, big men—and big risks, of course. Close your mouth, André. Good. Now, monsieur, I have a proposition to make to which you will agree. Notice, André, the use of the little word will, it establishes authority."

Paul sat there, certain that he could not lot these men steal the money. Elise would give him hell if he did. The money was to go to Sister Thérèse—all of it.

"And the proposition?" asked Paul.

"The six million in the safe is yours. But for the time being I keep the key. I shall give you the key when we have made another six million for me."

"And how are we to make it?"

"We do it quickly in one go In fact we begin today. In this town, monsieur, you may not know, but there is a very rich old man who gives his money away. Monsieur Durobat he is called. You have heard of him?"

"I have," said Paul faintly.

"Each afternoon he comes to the town. This afternoon we kidnap him, bring him here—and he pays a ransom of six million francs." Chrysantos beamed happily at Paul. "Observe, André, I am concise when it comes to the plan. Sharp, direct, no beating about the mulberry tree." Then to Paul, he said, "What do you say, Monsieur? Ah, I see you are overcome by the brilliance of my plan."

Paul stood up. "What do I think? … I think that at this moment we all need a drink."

"Excellent!" cried Chrysantos. "Notice, André— the moment of accord. The bargain to be sealed with this hospitable offer of refreshment. So civilised. Later, we shall choose our bedrooms and make ourselves comfortable here."

Paul smiled bleakly. "For the moment let's have a drink … He was moving to do something about it when a voice from the open doorway said:

"Don't bother, Paul, *cheri*, I'll get them." Elise was standing there. "I came back with your chauffeur whom I met in the town."

Chrysantos was on his feet and bowing, André gaped a little more and Monsieur Plume frowned and blinked. Their reactions were reasonable. The tribute of those who look on loveliness. She stood there beautiful and composed, in a gold dress, her dark hair shining, scarlet lips like soft petals and her eyes on Paul. "You heard?" said Paul.

"Everything," said Elise. "I think it is a wonderful. idea. Brilliant." She smiled at Chrysantos.

"Who is this?" asked Chrysantos admiringly. His heart was melting like candle-wax.

"She's … she's—"

"I'm his accomplice," said Elise easily. "We always work together." And then as she came into, the room and walked entrancingly towards the sidetable that held the drinks, she went on, "Remember, André—f you work a high-class racket, you must have a high-class accomplice."

"Charming ..." said Chrysantos, ravished. "Charming ... Oh, happy André ... what a morning, what an experience for you, for us all!" He bounded forward like a rubber ball to help Elise, whip Paul said weakly:

"Make mine a large dry Martini

It certainly was an experience. Paul could not deny that. He had to kidnap himself and find a six million franc ransom A wild ghost chase.

"It's difficult," he said to Elise. They were walking in the garden before lunch. Gringo and his two henchmen wore in the billiard room playing snooker. They weren't concerned with keeping an eye on Paul. If he liked to run out on them he was welcome. The six million francs in the safe would go to them.

"But not impossible," said Elise firmly. "That six million in the safe is going to the orphanage—and then we're going to Paris and raise a family."

"But how can I kidnap myself?"

"You won't. I shall kidnap you—with the help of Gringo. We'll bring you back here blindfolded and put you in the cellar. Then you can change back into your proper clothes, slip out through the grotto and into the house."

"But at any moment Gringo may go down to the cellar. There won't be anyone there. He'll expect the old man. to eat ... and then there will be the ransom arrangements to make."

"Of course, but I shall do all that. The first principle in kidnapping is to keep the contacts with the kidnapped as few as possible. Gringo will see that—"

"It'll be a wonderful object lesson for André, too. All right, they never know that the cellar is empty ... But what about the six million?"

"We shall have to think about that. Let's get the old man safely in the cellar first."

"You're wonderful. Anyone would think you'd been kidnapping people all your life."

And Paul went on thinking she was wonderful. Halfway through a lunch, pleasantly punctuated by Gringo's tips on etiquette to André ("A bad mannered crook, Andre, can only operate in a working class milieu. The big money is in the finger-bowl and one-napkin-a-meal set") Elise took charge and not even Gringo had any criticism to make.

Late every afternoon before leaving the town Monsieur Durobat was in the habit of taking an aperitif at the *Dauphin Vert*. Elise was to get into conversation with him there and then offer to drive him home. They would go off in the car and, just outside the town, Gringo, hidden in the back, would reveal himself and blindfold the old man. Then he would be brought to the villa and marched down to the cellar. After that only Elise would have contact with him. While all this was going on Paul and Monsieur Plume and André would establish sound alibis. Paul would go off to tea with Signora Busoni and the other two spend the afternoon bathing on the beach at the little cove.

"Perfect," said Gringo, beaming at Elise. Then to Paul, he declared, "you are lucky to have such a partner. Brains and beauty. Note that, André, it's a formidable combination."

Paul nodded. "She took a lot of training, though. When she first came to me ... she was raw and gauche ... No dress sense, no *savoir faire*—"

He broke off with a wince as Elise kicked him under the table.

"So ... ?" mused Gringo. "We must compare our training schedules sometime."

"Money," said Monsieur Plume hollowly. "How do we get the money out of the old gaga?"

"Later," said Gringo. "We fix that when he is in the cellar."

"He must have a bed in the cellar. Every comfort," said Elise. "I shall need help fixing the place up."

"We shall do it together," said Gringo and the trio of gold teeth flashed as he smiled gallantly at her.

The kidnapping went like a dream.

"Sweet ..."

Gringo kept saying it to himself as he and Elise drove home. Monsieur Durobat alongside her was blindfolded and dignified. Gringo kept his revolver pressed between the old man's shoulder-blades and couldn't control a conversational urge.

"You are immensely wealthy, monsieur, I believe?"

"Immoderately so, yes."

"You understand what is happening to you?"

"But of course."

"We put your value at six million francs. A bagatelle for you."

"You won't get a sou out of me."

"We shall see."

That evening—with a phantom Monsieur Durobat locked up in the cellar—the party at the villa was quite gay. In fact Gringo and his two friends were more than a little gay. Champagne and the prospect of easy money had gone to their heads. Gringo, entirely captivated by Elise, pursued her with elephantine gallantries and it was while he watched this exhibition that an idea came to Paul. Later he got Elise alone in the garden. "You've made quite a hit with Gringo."

"That's true. He's already suggesting that if I get tired of working for you he would be delighted to give me a job."

"I'll knock his head off."

He put arms round her and kissed her. Elise sighed. He kissed her again.

Then he said, "I've an idea how we can get that six million out of the safe and give these people the slip. But it depends on you."

"Tell me."

Paul did and the next morning began a period of stalemate so far as Monsieur Durobat was concerned.

Elise coming up from the cellar after taking the old man breakfast reported to the party that he refused to say where he lived and he refused to countenance any question of paying them money.

"He says he's quite happy to spend the rest of his life in the cellar."

"I don't blame him," said Paul. "There's enough drink there to last a lifetime."

"Obstinate," said Monsieur Plume. "Maybe, Gringo, I should twist his arm a little," suggested André.

"No, André … He is old and a Chevalier of the, Legion of Honour. We are not monsters—yet. No, no, we shall starve him a little to begin with. He is used to eating well."

So they starved Monsieur Durobat for a day and a half and at the end of that tune Elise re ported:

"He says he can live on his fat for another week. He is quite happy with champagne and brandy."

"We must move tke drink," said Monsieur Plume.

"Impossible," said Paul. "It would take two days to do it and Elise couldn't do it alone. That means he would see us and be able to recognise us later."

"Quite right," said Gringo. "Remember, André, anonymity is the foundation of all kidnapping. For mademoiselle here, it is different. A beautiful face is harder to trace than an ugly one. She dyes for hair red, changes her lipstick and goes to Italy for a couple of months. No, here we are up against be courage of a true Frenchman."

"I twist his arm, maybe," suggested André.

Gringo shook his head. "Always with you, André, it is too much or too little. What is a twist of the arm at this stage?

A mosquito bite. No, mademoiselle, you tell him that if tomorrow he does not co-operate we shall cut off one of his ears."

"Who's going to cut it, off?" asked Paul.

Gringo smiled. "Why, André, of course. It will mark the end of his apprenticeship. Just think, André—" he patted the youth on the shoulder, "—your first ear."

André looked a little pale, gulped and said, "The left or the right?"

"The right," said Gringo.

But the next morning Elise reported:

"He says that it is of no consequence. He is beyond the age where his looks are important. But he insists that you use a sharp knife."

"A man of spirit,"' said Gringo admiringly. "André, you had better spend the morning sharpening your knife. Maybe when sees we mean business he will change his mind,"

André gulped and said, "Maybe it, is too great an honour for me ... Maybe, Gringo, I am not sufficiently experienced yet—"

"Nonsense, André. Every man is a little nervous until the moment comes—"

"Sure," said Paul, "I remember my first ear. I had rats in the tummy until I started—and then everything was all right."

"It doesn't bleed—not so much as you imagine," said Monsieur Plume hollowly.

"Of course not," said Gringo stoutly. "And after that, Monsieur Plume shall have the left ear, if necessary."

Elise gave Gringo a warm, admiring smile. "You are a man of iron ... It is good to work with someone of such strength of character. Ruthlessness in a man stirs a woman ..."

"Mademoiselle," Gringo gave a little bow, "beneath the iron is a core of softness ... a heart full of tenderness..." He took her hand and kissed it.

Ten minutes later as Elise strolled by herself on the terrace above the sea Gringo came out to her. He presented her with a rose and kissed her hand again.

"Sweet..." he said. "The morning is beautiful, the bright flowers, the blue sea and you, mademoiselle, like a jewel amidst them all. In you I recognise the woman I have been looking for all my life ..."

"And now you have found me?" She glanced at him coquettishly.

Gringo roiled his eyes in delight. "Poor André, poor Plume and poor Paul … such subtlety is beyond them. You and I, Mademoiselle Elise, operate on a higher plane. We understand one another without words."

"Let's use words for a while, anyway … Kyro."

Gringo sighed like a leaky boiler. "Kyro, … Elise … two notes of music …" "Words," said Elise. "Not music."

Gringo came back to earth and said shrewdly, "What is your proposition?" "Meaning?"

"That no man, no matter what his age, wants his ear cut off. The left or the right. Monsieur Durobat, I am sure, was in a reasonable frame of mind, You were a long time with him and when you appeared you had a tiny smile in the corner of your lips … It is there still. Your proposition, Elise."

"You are very clever, Kyro," said Elise.

"And you are very beautiful, Elise. Tell me what you plan."

"It might be a little dishonest."

"Admirable."

"And involve betraying your friends."

"Excellent …"

"Paul will be heartbroken."

"He will get over it."

"We should have to become equal partners."

"Sweet ... It is my ambition. Explain."

"You have the key of the safe?"

"Of course." He patted a pocket.

"You would be waiting by the little cove in an hour with six million francs?"

"Nothing easier... I see a whole new life opening before me."

"Us."

"A thousand apologies. Us."

"I have a cheque ..." For a moment Elise's hand slipped inside the front of her blouse and a piece of paper was waved like the flight of a large blue butterfly in front of Gringo's nose, "... for six million francs, drawn by Monsieur Durobat on a Marseille bank. We could have cashed it before mid-day."

"Charming! Superb! I see a golden future for us..." Gringo stretched out his arms for her, but Elise slipped aside gently.

"Let us not rush the preliminaries, Kyro. Our feet must be firmly on the pathway to the golden future first. In an hour at the little cove. *Entendu?*"

"I shall be there..." He beamed at her. "Ah, what an object lesson this will be to André never to trust anyone. His father is certainly getting his money's worth."

A few moments later Elise entered Paul's bedroom. She said triumphantly, "It worked."

"Good," said Paul, and then with a frown asked, "Did he kiss you?"

Elise smiled, "Would it matter?"

"Of course. I've noticed a tendency in you always to overplay a part ..."

"*Petit cochon* ... I like you to be jealous. But enough. In one hour. You must now get into your Monsieur Durobat clothes. The moment we get rid of Gringo we drive to the convent and give Sister Thérèse the money—"

"And then heigh-ho for Paris!" Paul suddenly grabbed her by the waist and swung her round. "You know," he said as he kissed her and set her down. "I've a feeling that we should open an antique shop in Paris. Those little Hermes figures of yours would go very well, and maybe—"

Elise put her hand on his mouth. "In Paris we work and we live honestly."

"Sure," said Paul. "We get our feet firmly on the golden pathway to an honest future." He grinned.

"Ah, so—you were watching and listening from the window. *Ma foi*. I can see that I shall have a jealous husband."

"Jealous of every hair on your head, every word you say to another ..." He kissed her again. "You're, wonderful. What an object lesson you will be to André—and Gringo— never to trust a woman ..."

There was no trouble at all. Gringo, a symphony in dove-grey was waiting at the roadside by, the cove. Elise drew up by him in Paul's car and he got in alongside her.

"You have the money?" she asked. "Of course."

"Show."

Gringo chuckled. "A woman after my own heart. What poise, what lack of trust, what perfect understanding ... We shall travel far." He pulled a thick packet of notes from inside his coat.

"You've got it wrong," said Paul, rising from under a dust sheet in the back of the car. "You're not travelling any distance." Gringo half turned, saw Monsieur Durobat towering above him, and then a rubber blackjack hit him behind the ear and the subsequent proceedings interested him no more.

"You know," said Paul as he and Elise lifted Gringo out and laid him beneath a clump of pines, "I've never used one of those things before. They really work. I suppose I haven't killed him?"

Gringo groaned and above the wash of the sea they heard him deep in coma say, "Sweet ..."

"Count the money," said Elise as they got back into the car and began to drive off. It was all there.

But when they got to the orphanage they couldn't find Sister Thérèse. In fact they couldn't find anyone but the lodgekeeper and he told them that the whole orphanage had gone off that morning for its annual outing to a small town in the hills about twenty miles inland.

"Of course," said Paul to Elise as they left the place. "I should have remembered. I gave Sister Thérèse a subscription for the outing a week ago. Well, there's nothing to do but drive up there. It's on the way to Paris—"

"But what about all my things?"

"Your brother can. bring them later. We can't hang about this town. Just. think what will happen when Gringo recovers."

He started the car and began to drive out of town. As he went he sang happily and Elise drew close to him and contemplated blissfully the years that lay ahead of her, listening to his tuneless singing.

They couldn't know it, of course, but the trouble was not to come from Gringo. It was to come from a quite different quarter. Half an hour after they had left the villa Madame Fouret arrived in a taxi from the station. She had left her sister comfortably installed at Aix-les-Bains. She found André and Monsieur Plume playing billiards and at once light warfare broke out between them. She refused to believe that such types could be guests of Monsieur Paul. And Monsieur Paul couldn't be found.

"We're working with him," said André, conscious of unwanted responsibility and trying to remember all his lessons. "But I don't see where you figure."

"Maybe she's his mother;" said Monsieur Plume.

But before the scene could really develop and put André right out of his depths there was an interruption.

A short, dapper, elderly figure in a white suit and a bad temper came bouncing into the room.

"Madame Fouret!" he shouted. "What the devil goes on here? Strange servants, a man staggering about my drive who looks as though he's drunk and says he's a guest here—and these." He glared at André and Monsieur Plume through his monocle.

"Monsieur le Comte," said Madame Fouret faintly.

And it was; Comte d'Auxier unexpectedly back from America and already confusedly aware that things were not right. Monsieur Plume, taking over Gringo's role manfully, said, "André—when a situation is confused and trouble brews, retire from it."

They both. slipped out while the Count was still. bellowing and dancing round the room. Half an hour later the situation was less confused. The police in town were seeking Monsieur Paul Ashcroft, impostor, and already the information had come to hand that Monsieur Ashcroft's car had been seen heading out of town on the Paris road. A police car was soon following it. And following the police car was Count d'Auxier with Madame Fouret.

"This man," fumed the Count, "he uses my house, he sleeps in my bed, he drinks my drink—"

"Oh, no, monsieur. He ordered his own—"

"He's a rogue!"

"He had such nice manners … and so English."

"Never trust the English!" the Count bellowed.

And ahead of them the police radio car, with a couple of motor cyclists preceeding it, was picking up messages from headquarters as the progress of Paul's car was relayed to it.

And away ahead of them all, Paul and Elise were just driving into the little town of Col-des-Pins with its pine trees and its waterfalls, its grotto and the cool tree-shaded pleasure gardens where the orphans under the care of Sister Thérèse were filling the resin-scented air with happy shouts.

To make the day a superlatively happy one for Sister Thérèse she suddenly looked up and saw Monsieur Durobat coming across the pine needles towards her. He was smiling and waving his silver-headed cane to some of the children who had recognised him.

"They are always glad to see you, monsieur," said Sister Thérèse.

"Sister," Monsieur Durobat raised his hat, gave her a little bow, and then handing a small brown paper packet to her, said, "I am on my way back to Paris. But before I leave ... Well, Sister, there is no need for a long speech ..."

And there wasn't because Sister Thérèse, the packet in her hand, was well able to recognise the crisp crackle that carne from it. "For the baths and the kitchens, Sister ... for the children."

"Ah, monsieur—"

"Not a word more."

Monsieur Durobat bowed again and then was moving away through the pines. Sister Thérèse opened the packet and with shaking fingers began to count the notes ...

Back in the car Elise said to Paul, "And now?"

"Into the town. There is a little hotel in the main square. I shall change there and then we will be on our way. This is goodbye to Monsieur Durobat."

"After a time, you will not miss him, I promise," said Elise. Paul gave her a smile and squeezed her hand.

It was a wide, cool square, lined with acacia trees and surrounded by pink and white buildings, a couple of cafes, a barber's shop, a urinoir and the Hotel des Pins. In the centre of the square was a large fountain, and a statue of some obscure French politician on which pigeons roosted.

Paul parked the car outside the hotel. Leaving Elise he took his suitcase from the boot and went into the hotel.

He booked a room with a bath and a few minutes later was happily peeling off the beard and disguise of Monsieur Durobat. In a little while he would walk out into the cool square, Paul Ashcroft for good, ready to face the world with Elise on his arm. With a girl like Elise it shouldn't be hard to live almost as honestly as any other man. Anyway a price had to be paid for happiness—and a family, apparently.

Down below, Elise, bored with sitting in the car, got out and strolled across the square. On the far side was a little wooden gateway and a path through some pines. At the side of the gate was a notice extolling the beauties of a natural grotto. Some cyclists came racing up to the gate as she stood there. They propped their bicycles together and, chattering like a flock of starlings, swept through the gate in a flurry of long bare legs and brief shorts. She began to stroll back across the square. She was happy. Not simply because she was in love and going to be married. One needed more than that. She had a man who needed changing. She would make a new man of Paul ... an honest man. It was the kind of work every woman relished. He needed a firm hand. She had one. She had two. Long, shapely, pretty hands—but firm.

And then the cool, peaceful square suddenly erupted. One minute the dogs were sleeping happily in the sunshine by the fountain and a few people were lazily sipping drinks under the red and yellow and green and blue awnings, and the next ... a volcano, a noisy, colourful turmoil. A police-car came sweeping into the square. Motor-cycles were roaring. Another car appeared, its horn blowing furiously to clear a growing crowd. And all at once there were shouts, cries, arms waving in the air, children running, shopkeepers at their doors, and the pigeons going up from the statue in a great *clack, clack* of wings. And the vortex of it all was Paul's car outside the hotel.

A policeman bellowed, "*Ou est-il? Ce monsieur anglais?*"

"His car! His car!" From Madame Fouret.

"He slept in my bed! The scoundrel! Arrest him!" From the Count.

"Impossible, monsieur le Comte, until we find him," from the police.

"What is it?"

"*Qu'est-ce que c'est?*"

"Who is it?"

"He is English. A crook."

"Ah, the English. Vive la France!"

"Where is he?"

And the question was answered by Madame Fouret.

"There be is!" she cried and pointed to the top of the steps running up to the hotel door. And the moment she had shouted she regretted it, for she was at heart very fond of Paul. But it was too late.

Paul stood at the top of the steps. He wore a straw boater, a neat grey suit, and a bowtie as bright as a tropical butterfly. One hand rested lightly on the silver head of a walking stick. He was whistling gently. The day was fine, the sky was blue—and Life, he was thinking, was good.

The thought lasted exactly three seconds.

A crowd of people rushed up the steps towards him, a crowd headed by three policemen, the Count, and Madame Fouret, and followed by a fine old ragtag and bobtail of lawabiding citizens determined to miss no fun though they were far from clear what it was all about.

"*Assassin!*"

"*Voleur!*"

"Perfidious Englishman!"

"*Communiste!*"

"Monster!"

"*De Gaulliste!*"

And somewhere faint in the roar the chirp of a young girl who sold souvenirs in the gift shop by the grotto, "But he is charming ..."

Paul saw Madame Fouret and the Count and (recalling a photograph of the Count he had seen in the villa) his mind signalled, "All is discovered." He began to run to the left along the terrace that fronted the hotel.

And from the middle of the square, helpless, Elise watched him go. She had found love, she thought with anguish, only to see it torn to pieces before her eyes by an angry crowd. She started after the crowd, her dark eyes blazing, and picking up Paul's stick which he had dropped she know that unless a miracle happened she was going to be arrested for striking a policeman. However ... maybe they would let her and Paul share the same cell.

But Paul, heavy though the odds were against him, had no intention of going to prison. He vaulted over the end of the terrace into the square and slipped through pavement tables and into a Cafe. As he went through the proprietress screamed at him. Going out of the rear door he heard the crowd crash into the place like a tidal wave. He ran down the back of some houses, chose a door and found himself racing through a barber's shop to the square again. He had a quick glimpse of a half-lathered face, saw a razor brandished, heard a cry of "Martha, check the till. We've been robbed!" and he was out into the square. Behind him there was another roar and then the rich sound of glass breaking and chairs being overturned. He headed across the square knowing that it was no good to take to open country. He had to find a place to hide … Otherwise, no Elise, no Paris, no family …

He slipped through the gift shop, raced along the side of a stream, swung left down an alley, ducked between the cars in a garage and came out opposite the urinoir. And wherever he went the crowd thundered after him, not gaining but not losing on him and spreading destruction and chaos in its wake. Within ten minutes haul was hot and almost breathless and one third of the buildings around the square had suffered. Then, as haul came charging round the corner of a little church, he saw Sister Thérèse, indifferent to all the noise and disturbance, walking calmly up the steps of the hotel. In that moment the obvious idea for salvation came to him.

He headed across the square, gained ten yards on his nearest pursuer, and was up the steps like a bounding gazelle.

He flashed by Sister Thérèse in the hall and went up the stairs three at a time. As he turned into the corridor where his room was he heard the crowd surge into the hotel below like a noisy rip tide and he felt the thunder of feet send a vast tramp and tremble through the building.

By the time he reached the door of his room he was already undressing, one hand ripping off his bow-tie, the other sending his boater skimming through the window at the far end of the passage.

In his room he slammed and looked the door and jumped for Monsieur Durobat's clothes and make-up which he bad left there. Paul had made quick changes before but never one as quick as this. At the end of most of his operations he had been forced to change quickly and move on, but this time ... Nemesis was even closer on his heels.

He could hear the shouting of voices and the slamming of doors as the search swept through the floor below his, and then as he fixed his beard and tidied his black cravat and kicked his own clothes under the bed be heard the thud of feet on the stairway.

He went to the door and stepped out. The, tide swept down on him led by the Count and a policeman. The count skidded to a stop before Paul and cried, "Monsieur, you have seen a young Englishman up here?"

"An Englishman?"

"Yes ... a thief, an impostor, he slept in my—"

"He wears a bow tie and a straw hat, monsieur!" panted the policeman.

"Ha ..." Paul's eyes brightened. "That is the young man. He came charging through my room, messieurs, like a veritable holocaust ... no, I mean whirlwind ... and out on to the balcony ... I was coming to complain. After all I am an old man and have come here for some peace, some rest—"

But he was talking to himself. The crowd was roaring by him into the room. Monsieur Durobat turned and went quietly to the head of the stairs.

He went down them slowly and in the hall he met Sister Thérèse on her way out. She greeted him with a warm smile. "I have just telephoned my convent, monsieur, to give them the good news. But tell me, monsieur, what is all that goes on here?"

"It is nothing, sister. Some local custom, no doubt."

He paused at the bottom of the steps and bowed to her. "Goodbye, sister."

She nodded her old apple head and beamed.

"Goodbye, monsieur. But surely you are no bicyclist at your age?"

Monsieur Durobat chuckled. Standing at the pavement's edge was Elise between two bicycles which she had taken from outside the grotto.

"Indeed I am, sister. My heart is young, and each day I take bicycling exercises with my niece here."

He took a bicycle, gave a little run and hopped into the saddle. Elise followed him and the two began to pedal across the square, their pace increasing with each moment they left the hotel farther behind. Sister Thérèse watched them benevolently. From inside the hotel a babble of sound was still going on. From the far side of the square came the gay, and curiously young whistling of Monsieur Durobat telling the world that it still owed him a living— and, unless he could wriggle out of it, he was going to make it honestly with the young girl at his side.

THE GOLDINI BATH

IT had been a long drive from Rome, and a tiresome one. Twice the lorry had given trouble; once with a puncture and then with dirt in the carburettor. John Mallet was hot and hungry and, worst of all, lost. All he knew was that he was somewhere in the Umbrian hills north of Lake Bolsena, that the late autumn sun was sinking rapidly, and that for the last half-hour he hadn't seen a signpost marked Roccasparta, which was the name of the small hill town he was making for.

The lorry bumped and rattled along the rough road. To his right a little stream, sunken by drought, crept along in the shade of tall chestnuts and to the left patches of vines and olives patterned the steep hillside like a grey and green quilt. A herd of black goats bounded unexpectedly out of the bushes ahead of him and streamed across the road, John braked violently and came to a stop. A peasant, jacket over his shoulder, stepped out of the bushes and grinned at John. He was old, his face a mass of wrinkles and he hadn't a tooth in his head.

John leaned out of the cab window and shouted in Italian: "I'm looking for Roccasparta."

The old man came up to the cab and eyed John carefully. "Roccasparta?"

"That's it. I want the Villa Goldini."

The old man nodded again, and said, "You speak Italian strangely. Americano, maybe?"

"No. Canadian. Am I O.K. for Roccasparta?"

"I have a brother who went to America. Many of the men from these parts go to America. But never Canada. It is not so rich, maybe? We are very poor around here."

John reached into his pocket and pulled out a hundred lire note. He handed it to the old man and said firmly: "Roccasparta, papa. Where is it?"

The old man examined the note carefully and John waited patiently. The westering sun struck through the trees and fired little glints of copper in John's untidy hair. He was twenty-four and had one of those brown, easy-going faces that smile more readily than they frown. He lit himself a cigarette and, seeing the old man's eyes on his movements, gave him one.

The peasant grinned and said, "My brother is dead now, of course. He never came back. Why should anyone? This is a poor country."

"Roccasparta," said John firmly.

"Ah, yes … Follow this road for five kilometres, take the turning to the left and then at the top of the hill go right. After that you cannot be mistaken."

John thanked him and moved off, edging the lorry through the black goats. They moved slowly out of his way. Everything and everybody moved slowly in this country, he thought. Money might mean something to them, but Time certainly didn't. Well, he was glad he wasn't an Italian. He liked to be up and doing. At his age there was a whole stack of things waiting to be done.

He followed the old man's directions carefully. But at the top of the hill the lorry broke down again, great plumes of steam spouting from the radiator cap. He found that the fan belt had broken. With a pair of pliers and some wire he spliced the broken ends together and refitted the belt. It was a simple job but it took him time and while he worked he cursed the Italian in Rome who had hired him the lorry.

It was dark when he moved off again. He switched his headlights on. The road ran downhill and on the corner the lights picked up a signpost. Pointing ahead it read— *Lago di Nello*—and backwards, the way he had come, it said—*Capena*. No mention of Roccasparta. John addressed a few angry words aloud to the Italian nation.

At the bottom of the hill the headlights fanned across a wide sweep of water. Little clumps of reeds broke the surface here and there. The road, rougher now, ran along the verge of the lake. Some way along it forked, one branch of the fork running away from the lake and up the hillside. John drew up and got out. There was no signpost on the fork. He stood there in the headlights, frowning. Which way was he to go? At that moment, tired and hungry, he felt that he would never reach Roccasparta.

As he walked round to the cab of the lorry he saw through the trees at the lakeside the glimmer of a light. He left the lorry and made his way towards it. A light meant life and, maybe, he could get directions. He only hoped that they would be more reliable than the old man's.

The light came from the small window of a wooden cabin built under the trees at the top of the narrow lake beach. John knocked on the door, but there was no answer. He knocked three or four times and then pushed the door open and went in.

The cabin held one room, lit by a smoking oil lamp on the window sill. On a wooden table were three of four flasks of *chianti*, half a loaf and a piece of cheese. An empty flask was lying on the floor close to a camp bed on which a man lay stretched out and snoring gently.

John went up to him. He was a man of about thirty-five with short black curly hair and a fat, round face smudged with a neat little moustache. There was a gleam of gold teeth as he snored his mouth sagging open. He wore a flashy red and grey striped suit. and very pointed black shoes. And he was obviously very drunk. The whole place reeked of wine.

John shook him by the shoulder but he just rolled over irritably in his sleep. John tried again, but without success. He stood there for a moment, then he shrugged his shoulders and helped himself to some cheese and bread. While he ate he pulled his map from his pocket and tried to find Lago di Nello and Capena—but so far as the map was concerned they had no existence. He had another glass of wine and then went back to the man. He shook him and shouted in his ear—"Wake up!" The man smiled in his sleep and snored a little louder. John gave up.

He went back to his lorry, tossed a coin for it and took the road up the hill away from the lake. An hour later the road, which had slowly grown rougher and narrower, died away altogether and John found his headlights illuminating the steep sides of an old quarry. It was now nearly midnight. John gave up. Re turned the lights off, climbed into the back of the lorry and went to sleep under a tarpaulin.

He was awake early the next morning and washed himself at a small spring that rose close to one of the quarry walls. He was standing there towelling himself when he heard the sound of a shot behind him. Overhead came the whistle of pellets and then their sharp rattle against the walls of the quarry away to his left. Somebody called out and a brown and white dog raced by him and disappeared into the bushes at the foot of the rock face. A few seconds later the dog reappeared, a great grin over its face, holding a quail in its mouth. It walked by John without taking any notice of him and, as he turned to watch it, a girl came round the back of the lorry and bent to take the bird from the dog.

Buttoning his shirtfront John walked across to her.

"*Buon giorno*," he said, smiling.

She straightened up from the dog, and said "*Buon giorno*" and then she stood there looking at him curiously. She was little more than twenty, with dark, glossy hair that was drawn back over her head and caught with a red ribbon. She wore a yellow skirt, stained with moss and torn at the hem, a rough blue shirt, and she held a shotgun in the crook of her arm. She was very beautiful, thought John. But also she had a firm. chin and a straightforward look which spoke of character. Not the kind of girl, he decided, who would put up with any nonsense.

"That's a nice dog," he said.

"Bitch," she corrected him. "What are you doing here?"

"I'm looking for Roccasparta," he said. "Personally, I'm getting a feeling that it doesn't exist."

"It exists, all right," she said. "You're not Italian, are you?"

"No. Canadian. Do I speak the language so badly?"

"Well …"

John grinned. "I took a correspondence course while I was at McGill."

"McGill?"

"That's a university—in Canada."

"Oh, I see. Well, if you want to go to Roccasparta, I'll take you there …"

"You will?"

"Of course. It will save me the walk back."

"That's very nice of you." John hesitated for a moment, and then added, "I'm John Mallet."

"Gabriella Mondovi," she said.

A few minutes later, with the dog between them in the cab of the lorry, John was driving back alongside the lake. They went up the hill and there took a turning which he had not noticed the previous night.

"Roccasparta is about four kilometres further along this road," said Gabriella. "But people do not usually come into it this way. Are you going to stay there?"

"Not for long. I have a job to do there, but I shouldn't think it would take much time." He turned and grinned at her. "You see, I'm collecting a bath."

"You're what?" Surprise was clear in her voice. John grinned. It was a lovely morning. He was going to get to Roccasparta this time, and he had a charming companion. He felt expansive.

"Sounds crazy, doesn't it? But it isn't really. You see, when I left McGill after taking my engineering degree, I got a job with this chap Fuller. Never heard of him, I suppose? In Canada you would have done. He's in everything, oil, mines, engineering … pots of money. Took me on as a technical secretary … personal assistant, really. We've been five months in Europe. Business and pleasure. He's gone back now, but he sent me up for this bath. He's mad about antiques and stuff like that. Gosh, you ought to see his house. About the only thing it lacks is a gold bath and—"

"Do you mind stopping this lorry?"

Her voice came cold and cutting.

John looked at her in surprise. "What's the matter? Have I said something?"

"Please. Stop this lorry."

Frowning, John brought the lorry to a stop. "Say, what have I done? I didn't even try to hold your hand ..."

She jerked open the door of the cab and jumped down to the road and the dog followed her. For a moment she looked up at him. Her face was serious and there was a determined little twist to her mouth.

"I have nothing against you personally, Signore Mallet— but if you take my advice you will not go to Roccasparta. It could be very uncomfortable for you. Also," and the note of pride was clear in her voice, "—I would rather die than ride into Roccasparta with you."

She turned, and with the dog at her heels, made her way briskly into the trees at the edge of the road and disappeared.

Well ... what was this all about, John asked himself? And just when they were getting on so well. What was the matter with this crazy country?

He sat there for a moment, staring at the trees. Then, with a shrug of his shoulders, he started the lorry. He didn't know why things might be uncomfortable for him in Roccasparta—but he knew this; if he returned to Mr. Fuller without the bath life would be even more uncomfortable for him. Mr. Fuller was used to getting what he wanted.

The road wound up to Roccasparta like a corkscrew. Perched at the top of a sugar-loaf hill was a collection of redroofed houses and the grey towers of a church, all grouped around a small square, uneven with cobbles, and fringed with falsepepper trees. The place looked hot and dead. John drew the lorry up outside the *Albergo Nationale*—to which he had sent a telegram booking a room. He went into the hallway. There was no one at the untidy reception desk. The place was so silent he could have heard a pin drop. Everywhere there was a smell of garlic and fresh-baked bread. He looked into the dining room. Empty. The lounge. Empty. He walked through into the back of the, hotel to the kitchens and the service. The place was deserted.

He came back to the hall, and as he stood there he heard the sudden sound of a rich burst of cheering from somewhere in the square. He went out to the lorry. The square seemed empty. Then he heard the cheering again and across by the church he saw the dark stir of a crowd clustered about the shallow steps that led up to the great arched entrance to the church.

Curious, he walked across the square and now, as he got closer, he saw that a mass of people was clustered on the steps … Men, women and children … housewives, cooks, shopkeepers, the whole boiling. At the top of the steps stood a priest in cassock and biretta and by his side the Roccasparta *carabiniere*. The priest was speaking but his Italian was too rapid for John to follow it.

Edging into the crowd a little John touched a young man on the shoulder and asked politely, "What is happening? What's it all about?"

Almost without turning the young man said, "It's Silvestro. He has had a splendid night."

"Silvestro?"

The young man turned and gave him a quick look. Then he smiled. "He has had a good night at the Casino. We now have ten million lire. Another couple of nights and, with luck, we shall have the fifteen. Ah, what a man is Silvestro … he has the hand, the cunning, and the experience."

"I don't understand."

"It is simple. He has lived in America. He is used to big money. Ah, *bello Silvestro*, the one who is to save Roccasparta … and to think he started three weeks ago with only ten thousand lire—"

At that moment the priest gave the crowd his blessing and it broke around John like a flood as the people turned back to their homes and their occupations. A cook went by him with a ladle in his hand, the schoolchildren formed up in flying crocodile and rushed away behind the chinch, and in the hustle John was forced back into the square. He felt a little dazed. Things were really beyond him.

He went into the hotel again. A fat man in shirt sleeves with steel-rimmed spectacles pushed up above his eyes sat at the desk. The clanging of pans came from the kitchen quarters. A waiter was shouting in the dining room, and four men were playing cards in the lounge.

The man at the desk looked up at John and said, "Signore?"

John said, "I telegraphed for a room from Rome. Mallet is the name."

The man stood up as though he had been stung. "Signore Mallet? Happily, signore—we have no rooms."

"Happily? No rooms?"

"No rooms, signore. And the other three hotels, happily have no rooms."

The man was smiling, and behind the smile John could sense a defiance and triumph. He felt that he was being given the run-around and his lips tightened. From the corner of his eye he saw the four card players in the lounge watching him, legs asprawl, and the same kind of smile on their faces.

Stubbornly, John said, "I'm not interested in the other hotels. I telegraphed for a room here four days ago. If you hadn't got a room you should have had the courtesy to reply. Since you didn't—you'll please find me a room!"

Just for a moment the proprietor weakened. This redheaded young man with the pugnacious jaw and the angry flecks of yellow in his brown eyes looked as though he might step forward and use force. Then, conscious of the card-players and the waiter watching him, the proprietor found new courage.

"Impossible, signore. We are full. Also—I did not receive any telegram from you."

"Don't give me that! You know you did—" John stepped forward, but as he moved a hand fell gently on his shoulder. He spun round and found himself facing the priest who had been on top of the church steps. He had a long intelligent face and the corners of his mouth were kinked with the hint of some inner amusement. He looked strong and capable and yet there was a suggestion of patient gentleness about him.

"Rosario," said the priest, addressing the proprietor, "it is a bad thing for the soul, and for business, to misinform this young man about your rooms. You meant well, Rosario, but it is not necessary to go so far. Give me the key to room 7."

He turned to John. "The room has a fine view of the square. I will show it to you."

"But, Father Fabiano—"

Father Fabiano cut Rosario's protest short with a wave of his hand and said sternly, "The key."

The key was handed over and Father Fabiano, with a little bow, led John up the stairs.

John stood at the window of his room, looking out over the sunlit square towards the facade of the church. Behind him Father Fabiano was speaking.

"It is very easy to understand, my son. You see, Roccasparta is a small place and the people here are very poor. Only one thing brings them prosperity—and that is the gold bath at the Villa Goldini. During the summer tourists come from all over the world to see it, and they stay here in one or other of the four hotels, and they spend money on souvenirs. Without the bath ... well, Roccasparta would be forgotten and become even poorer. Naturally, then, you are not welcome, since you come to take it away."

John turned round. "But if that's so, the man to blame surely is Count Goldini for selling it? He's the one they should go for."

"No. The Count is one of us. Also, too, he is very poor— otherwise he would not wish to sell this magnificent bath which has been in his family for generations. It was made, you know by an artist who learnt his craft from the great Benvenuto Cellini "

"Yes, I know that. But the Count has agreed to sell. He had many telephone conversations with my employer, Mr. Fuller. The price has been agreed. Fifteen million lire and I—Oh ..." John paused and looked shrewdly at the priest. "Now, that's funny. Fifteen million ..."

Father Fabiano smiled. "I saw you in the crowd at the church. You are thinking of Silvestro?"

"Yes. Just what goes on there?"

"It is very simple, my son. The Count is a good man—though a little eccentric. If there is a way to keep the bath in Roccasparta, and also to provide him with the fifteen million lire he wants, he would like that to happen. So, we, the people of Roccasparta, collected ten thousand lire for Silvestro … Everyone, man, woman and child gave what they could. Silvestro has gone off to the Casino—"

"I see. And he's trying to raise the wind? Gambling. Do you approve of that?"

"No, my son, I do not. But I do not approve of the people of Roccasparta becoming poorer than they are. Count Goldini has given them a month to find the money. There are still six days to go. If Silvestro is successful the Count will sell the bath to the town—"

"But he said nothing of this to Mr. Fuller. I'm up here to hand over a cheque and collect the bath."

"Maybe the count forgot to mention it. Maybe he did not think Silvestro would be so lucky."

"Well, Mr. Fuller's not going to like this way of doing business. I'd better get up to the villa and see the Count. If Mr. Fuller doesn't get that bath! You've no idea, Father, how he's set his heart on it."

Father Fabiano fished in a pocket of his gown and pulled out a key. "The Count is away until tomorrow, but this is one of the keys to the bathroom. He asked me to give it to you so that you might examine the bath if you wished before his return."

"Well, I'd certainly like to have a look at it."

"Naturally, my son. The villa is on the road that goes down the hill behind the church. About five minutes from here. But if you will accept a little advice from me, I suggest you wait until this evening. Until my people get used to the idea of your being here I should not go out in broad daylight. We have, you know, like all other places, a few hot-heads. Just be polite and natural, my son, and—" he glanced at John's red hair, "—on no account lose your temper."

John grinned. "I'll try not to. But my mother was Irish."

Father Fabiano nodded. "The Irish. Ah, yes. When I was a young man at theological college we had Irish students ... Yes, I remember them well."

Left alone, John unpacked his case. Mr. Fuller was back in Canada now. But he'd left him with a tricky mission. If in the next six days Silvestro turned his ten million lire into fifteen million (and he had done very well so far, considering he'd started with only ten thousand) then the bath would stay in Roccasparta. Mr. Fuller's reaction to that would be violent. Any hopes, he, John, had of moving on from being the old man's assistant to a good engineering job would fade ... No, somehow or other, the bath had to go to Canada. It was just bad luck for the people here. The real culprit was Count Goldini ... After all, he didn't have to sell it. He could stay poor like the rest of his people.

At lunch John was given a small table and pushed up in a corner close to the kitchen entrance. The waiter served him with the minimum of words and the maximum of delay. He was treated as though he were a leper who had only himself to blame for contracting his disease. Remembering Father Fabiano's instructions, John kept his temper. His coffee was served to him, barely lukewarm, in the lounge and outside the window which looked on to the square a small knot of people collected and watched him. He was a young man with a great deal of selfconfidence, but he began to feel like an animal in the zoo. He turned his back on the crowd and started to read an old magazine.

A shadow fell across the pages and a voice speaking English with a heavy French accent said, "You are being remarkably, patient, *mon ami*. I admire you. In your place I would have thrown the cold soup in the waiter's face, and the coffee pot through the window at the crowd outside. Pardon me, Alexis Castillot ..."

Standing over him was a short, plumpish, neat little man with an almost bald head and a pince-nez perched on the tip of a pudgy nose. He wore a white silk suit and a black cravat.

John smiled. "Thank you. But you'll be lynched if you are seen talking to me."

"Ah, no ..." Monsieur Castillot spread his hands. "I do not belong to either side. I am a writer, a dispassionate observer, yes. I compile guide-books for a Paris firm and my only interest is to stay a little while to see whether in our next edition we have to put a foot-note that the Goldini Bath has been sold to Canada ... Alas, I hope it does not happen. Such a great treasure should stay in its own country."

He stayed for a little while, chatting, and then with a smile and a quick bob of a bow, took his leave.

It was seven o'clock and the autumn dusk was drifting in a purple mist across the square when John left the hotel. A few people were sitting outside a cafe on the other side of the square. John moved unobtrusively away under the trees and took the road to the villa. He found it easily enough, but in the gloom it was difficult to make out much detail. Large, double gates of wrought iron fronted the road and a small drive went up through terraced gardens to the villa itself. The air was full of the scent of flowers and distantly there was the musical sound of a fountain playing.

A footman in a green tail-coat and white gloves opened the door and John handed him his card and explained his mission. The footman said, "The master is not at home, but we have instructions to allow you to examine the bath."

John was led across the hall, handed over to another footman and then conducted upstairs and through a maze of passages.

The footman stopped in front of a stout wooden door, bound with iron straps.

"You have a key, signore?"

"Yes."

"When you have finished please ring this bell—" he pointed to a bellpush in the wall, "and I will come for you." He glided away like a ghost into the gloom of the passageway.

John put the key in the lock. It opened easily and smoothly. He went through and the door, self-locking, clicked gently behind him. He was in a short passageway and another door faced him. He took the handle and opened it

A blaze of light streamed into the little passage and someone gave a surprised cry. For a moment John stood there blinking against the strong light. Then, as his eyes focussed, he stared open-mouthed.

Enclosed on three sides by tall mirrors was the great gold bath with little drifts of vapour rising from it. The bath set low in the floor glistened and shone under the lights. John had a swift impression of rich mouldings of birds and animals, graceful leaf scrolls and fruit—all in gold along the rim of the bath—and then he forgot all about the bath.

Standing up in it was a young girl with a large towel draped hurriedly about her body. John was vividly aware of damp, dark hair lying over bare shoulders, the flash of brown arms and legs, and the angry face of Gabriella Mondovi.

"Get out—you horrible Canadian!" she shouted. But before she had finished speaking John had slammed the door and was retreating down the passage.

Outside John found a chair in the gloomy passageway and sitting down lit a cigarette. His instinct was to ring for the footman and get out of the villa as soon as possible. But on the other hand he still wanted to have a look at the bath …

The heavy door from the bathroom corridor swung open and Gabriella came through. She reached out for a switch and suddenly the passageway was ablaze with light.

She stood there, wrapped in a large yellow towelling gown, and looked at him. Her lips were tight, but for a moment John thought he caught a flicker of amusement in her eyes and he took hope.

He stood up. "I'm very sorry," he said. "But the footman told me it was all right to go in."

"I understand," she said crisply. "It is not often the family use the bath."

"The family?"

"Count Goldini is my uncle. I live here."

"Oh, I see it all now."

"You see what?"

John smiled. "Well, I imagine from the way you jumped out of my lorry that you're on the Roccasparta-Silvestro side. Right?"

"I certainly am."

He nodded. "I'm sorry I can't be, too. But unfortunately I'm just here on a job. And my job is to take the bath to my employer. You can't blame me for that."

"Nobody is blaming you. But you can see that no one is exactly welcoming you with open arms..." She stepped aside and motioned to the door. "The bath is all yours—for the moment."

She was beautiful, John thought. It was wonderful what the yellow robe did for her dark hair. And she was reasonable, too, he decided. Very few girls had ever attracted his interest so much. If he had had to pick someone in Roccasparta to give him an open-arm reception it would have been her. Moving towards the door he said, "Why don't the family use the bath often?"

She smiled. "Because it is a show-piece. Conducted parties are in and out all day, during the season. Also because of the legend."

"Oh, there's a legend, is there?"

"Yes. Anyone who uses the bath only once a year can make a wish—"

"And it comes true?"

"Yes."

"Anyone? Not just the family?"

"Anyone."

"And what were you wishing just now when ..."

She gave a little frown. "If the wish is told then it won't come true."

He grinned. "I'll bet my Mr. Fuller wouldn't approve of your wish."

For a moment he thought she was going to reply. Then she gathered her robe around her and without another look at him went away down the passage, leaving a scented cloud behind her. John went back into the bathroom.

He knew nothing about antiques or the fine craft of goldsmiths, but the bath really impressed him. It was something that hit you straight in the eye. It was rather narrow and sunk almost to floor level in a wall recess, the three sides of which were made of large mirrors. The lower part of the bath shell inside was smooth, but from about half-way up a great band of decoration ran right round it and curled up to form the overhanging edges of the bath. It was a wonderful piece of work ... flowers, birds and beasts, carved and moulded and seeming to spring from the soft, yellow matrix of the bath. When you lay in it your head rested against a great embossed coat of arms of the Goldini family. It was almost a shock to see an ordinary nailbrush lying on its lip ... left by Gabriella, he guessed.

The water came into the bath through the mouths of two dolphins that sprang out of the far end of the bath in a graceful leap that the goldsmith had arrested in mid-air for all time. It really was some bath and, John realised, just the kind of thing Mr. Fuller would set his heart on.

He had a good look around it and saw—he was on more familiar ground now—that an hour's work would easily free the fittings. But he guessed that it would take three or four men to carry the thing. It depended on how thick the gold shell of the lower part of the bath was. He couldn't know this until it was moved.

Back in the passage he rang for the footman and was shown out.

He slept late the next morning and when a waiter brought him his coffee on a tray, there was a note with it from Count Goldini asking him to lunch that day. While he was shaving he heard the sound of people moving across the square and a confusion of angry voices ... an anonymous, grumbling note.

Leaning out of the window he saw that the people of Roccasparta were coming back from the church. Two or three of them, seeing him at the window, raised their fists and shook them at him. A voice called up to him from the pavement and he saw Monsieur Alexis Castillot.

"What's the trouble?" John asked. "I seem even more unpopular this morning."

"You are, *mon ami*," beamed Monsieur Castillot. "Silvestro has had a bad night. The morning bulletin is just in. He lost five millions off his ten million francs. And only five days to go. You'd better keep out of the way. Have you had your coffee yet?"

"Yes."

"A pity',,

"Why?"

"It may well have been poisoned." Monsieur Castillot grinned. "You feel quite well?"

John decided to keep out of the way. Later in the morning he slipped out and drove off in his lorry which he had parked at the back of the hotel. He went to the nearest town, five miles away, and sent a long cable to Mr. Fuller explaining the situation. Then he came back, avoiding Roccasparta, and went to the Villa Goldini for lunch.

They were four people there: Gabriella and Father Fabiano looking gloomy still from the bad Silvestro news; Monsieur Castillot beaming amiably and Count Goldini showing no emotion whatever.

The count was a tall man, as thin as a lathe, his shoulders slightly stooped, and he had a long, horsey face, a mouth full of very big teeth, and large soft eyes like a spaniel. He was well into his fifties, hair going white, and quite clearly most of the time his thoughts were far away from Roccasparta … but where they were it was doubtful if even he knew. John liked him but guessed at once that he was going to be a hopeless man to pin down.

They sat on a terrace that looked out over the gardens having their drinks before lunch.

"You are Canadian, they tell me," said the Count.

"That's right."

The Count nodded. "It is a country of opportunities. Here there are a no opportunities. New Zealand is also a country of opportunities. You understand about caponisation?"

"About what?"

"Caponisation. But I see you don't." He smiled and waved a hand over the gardens. "I cannot afford this place, you know. The only money I have is from the vines and the olives. But in New Zealand I should raise cockerels and caponise them. They grow fat and one sells them for a large profit. All my life I have wanted to make large profits ..."

"Who hasn't?" said Monsieur Castillot.

John said, "I have a cheque for fifteen million lire from Mr. Fuller in my pocket. If you will give me a receipt for it, I will take the bath and then you will be free to go to New Zealand."

"Why, of course," the Count held out his hand.

Gabriella stood up. "You can't do that, uncle. There is Silvestro."

"Yes, Silvestro ..." said Father Fabiano gently. "You remember?"

"Oh, of course. Silvestro. No, I cannot accept it yet." The Count smiled at John "I have this arrangement about Silvestro, you know."

"I know," said John. "But also, you made your bargain with Mr. Fuller first."

"Ah, Yes ... he is the gentleman who came here some time ago. He knew about caponisation. It was very interesting talking to him. How is he?"

Hopping mad, thought John, if he's got my cable yet. But he said, "Very well. But he would think it a little odd if he knew that you had made another bargain with the people of Roccasparta since making the one with him."

"Yes, of course. Very odd. Would you like another drink?"

"Thank you."

Gabriella brought it to him and just for a moment her lower lip curled and there was a glint of a smile in her eyes. All right, thought John, so I'm getting nowhere.

"But how shall I explain this oddness to him?" asked John diplomatically.

The Count shrugged. "Is it necessary? He is a business man. He must be used to odd bargains. Anyway in five days we shall know, shall we not, whether he gets the bath or it stays here?"

Somewhere in the house a gong sounded for lunch and John gave up. Going in to lunch Gabriella said lightly, "You like my uncle?"

"He's charming."

"But illogical?"

"That's one word for it. If Mr. Fuller doesn't get his bath he'll have another word for it—and I shall be out on my ear."

"What do you mean by that?"

"Nothing … just that if he didn't want me to have a job in Canada I shall probably end up in New Zealand chicken farming, too. I'd better start reading up about caponisation."

Gabriella smiled. "My uncle will lend you some books on it. Maybe you will like New Zealand."

"I'm sure I shall—if you're there with your uncle."

Behind him he heard Monsieur Castillot give a little giggle and Gabriella's small frown flashed across her forehead.

Well, there it was, John told himself. Five days to go for a decision and not a thing he could do except sit it out. And sit was the operative word because he wasn't tempted to do much strolling about Roccasparta. He began to have some idea of what it must be like to be the President of a Mid-European country whose every minute was marked with the fear of assassination. When the news from Silvestro was good he went into the square. When it was bad he stayed in the hotel. Sometimes he played gin rummy with Monsieur Castillot. Sometimes he just sat. Once or twice he got into the lorry and drove off and took a walk over the hills.

The morning after he sent his cable to Mr. Fuller he had a reply. It read—*Nowaphi jacks me. Bringbathbac kore lse*. He sorted it out, gloomily, wondering if the Roccasparta telegraph office had done it on purpose, to read—*No wop hijacks me. Bring bath back or else.*

The Silvestro news that morning was good—from a Roccasparta point of view. He was back to ten million lire.

The next morning (three days to go) Silvestro was up to twelve million. John had three drinks before lunch to cheer himself up and lost five hundred francs to Monsieur Castillot at gin rummy.

The next morning (two days to go) Silvestro was down to eight million lire. As John put his head out of the window to get the morning bulletin from Monsieur Castillot, a stone hit the wall a yard to his left. He withdrew, grinning. Downstairs Rosario, the hotel proprietor, his eyes bland behind his steel-rimmed spectacles announced that, owing to the rising cost of living, he was increasing his price by twenty-five per cent.

"That's okay chum," said John. "Mr. Fuller is paying."

Rosario said glumly, "You have a wife and family who will miss you, signore?"

"No."

"I have a wife, and six children ... without tourists this hotel will be kaput. Why can't your Mr. Fuller be content with an ordinary bath?"

"Search me."

"Maybe you could make him change his mind?"

John shook his head, "Not with a couple of bull-dozers. Anyway, cheer up. Silvestro may do better tonight."

"Ah, Silvestro ... we are cousins. He is a clever man. Very clever always ... always thinking of things. When he was a gangster in America ... always presents to all the family."

"A gangster?"

"That was years ago. Now he is respected and is retired to Rome."

The next morning (one day to go) Silvestro was up to fourteen million lire and there was an impromptu victory dance in the square. John was greeted with smiles everywhere until midday when another message came from the telegraph office saying there had been a mistake and the figure should read four million, not fourteen. John got congealed soup, gristly meat, vinegary wine and cold coffee for lunch. Gabriella, who was lunching with Monsieur Castillot at the hotel, never once looked in his direction. The only person who spoke to him all day was Father Fabiano.

He came up to his room at four in the afternoon and said, "My son, I have a feeling that Silvestro is going to fail. This is the last night. Because of this, I have persuaded the Count to let you sleep at the villa tonight. You will take your lorry up there, too. No one will do anything to you while you are in the villa."

"That's very nice of you, father. And believe me, I'm sorry about all this. But I have a job to do. What goes on here isn't anything I can help. In fact, if it, were just me, I'd leave the bath here."

"It is a complicated situation, my son. I presume you have acquainted Mr. Fuller with the facts?"

"I have. But there's no hope in that direction, father."

Father Fabiano smiled gently. "I imagine the word hijack means what I imagine it means, my son?"

"Sure, father. And it means double that when Mr. Fuller uses it."

"You have your work to do, my son. And a man must be faithful to his contracts … That is a lesson we all have to learn, Wops, Yankees, Limeys and Kanuks…"

John grinned.

When it was dark John got his lorry out and drove up to the villa. He parked it in the courtyard at the back of the house. He was shown to his room and then had dinner alone with Count Goldini. There was no sign of Gabriella. Half-way through dinner the Count said suddenly:

"She comes and goes, you know. I have no control over her. Really she lives in Rome. She is lucky to have escaped from Roccasparta. My family have been here too long. Italy has too many families that have been in the same place too long. The days of old families and gold baths is finished."

"It's tough on the people of Roccasparta, though."

"Of course. But all change is hard at first on someone. if I could afford it I would present the bath to Roccasparta and then go to New Zealand, but I cannot afford it. It is as simple as that."

Later in his room, John was just thinking of turning in when there was a knock on his door. In answer to his call Gabriella entered.

She stood just inside the door, looking very serious.

"Signore Mallet," she said, "I wish to speak to you."

"You can call me John."

"This is a serious matter. I am here on behalf of the people of Roccasparta."

"They couldn't have picked a more welcome delegate."

"Please attend. I have an ultimatum. You must leave Roccasparta with your lorry tonight or accept the consequences if—"

"If Silvestro fails?"

"If Silvestro fails. Believe me, we are quite determined to keep the bath here. We have nothing against you personally—"

"I'm glad to hear that."

"But if you try to remove the bath there will be trouble."

"I see." John moved over close to her. "And what would you advise me to do?"

"To go. For your own sake."

"And what do you think I shall do?"

He saw her lips quiver for a moment. Then she said quietly, "I think you will be a damn fool and stay. You are stubborn and determined and … and I told them you would be like this."

"You told them right, Gabriella. I can't run away. My feet aren't built that way. And what good would it do? Mr. Fuller would only send someone else—"

"Oh, Mr. Fuller!" She stamped her foot sharply. "I could—"

"Sure. So could I." He put out a hand and touched her arm. She let it rest there for just three seconds longer than he could have hoped for and then turned on her heels and left the room.

John undressed, whistling to himself, and slept like a dog.

If History were going to be made, thought John— and for an engineer he had quite a philosophical turn of mind—then it was hard to resist the impulse to be present; even when it was only local Roccasparta history. Common-sense told him that it would be wiser to be discreet, but the Irish in him over-ruled his head. The morning bulletin came in from Silvestro about half-past nine. At nine, John slipped quietly through the churchyard and into a small garden alongside the church steps. He had previously noticed in the garden a little three-sided bamboo summer structure. He hid himself in this and, pushing the bamboo slats aside a little, had a clear view of the church steps.

At a quarter to nine the people of Roccasparta began to gather at the church. He knew a lot of them by sight now. Rosario from the hotel with his cook; the *carabiniere* with a pretty girl who served behind the bar in one of the other hotels, the housewives, black-aproned and bare-armed and chattering like starlings, the schoolchildren in an orderly crocodile ... rapidly the crowd thickened about the steps. And there wasn't a face in the crowd which was lightened by hope. Yesterday Silvestro had been down to four million. There wasn't much chance John thought that he could have parleyed that into fifteen million in one night's play.

At nine-thirty Father Fabiano, who lived in a little house behind the church, came through the churchyard and mounted the steps. His people stood aside for him respectfully. John could see his face clearly. It was a calm mask. No one could have told what news he had. When he reached the top of the steps, he turned and looked down at his people, and then he smiled gently.

"*Buon giorno*, my children," he said.

There was a little murmur in response. At this moment, too, John with his face pressed against the bamboo slats heard a noise behind him. He glanced round. Standing in the entrance to the bamboo shelter was a tiny dog, a brown nondescript dog of no size and mixed ancestry, and with a suspicious curl to its lips. It cleared its throat officiously. The noise was not very convincing.

"Go away," hissed John and turned backs to the crowd.

"My children," Father Fabiano was saying, "I have three announcements to make. The first, you know already, but I repeat it. I do not approve of the method adopted to raise money for the Goldini bath. This is a matter of conscience which I shall take up with you all individually as the occasion arises—"

"Father, please, the news," piped a voice.

"Patience," said Father Fabiano. "My second announcement is that yesterday there was a second error in the telegraph message and it has now been made clear that Silvestro finished the night not with four or fourteen million, but with eight million—"

A cheer greeted this, and the dog behind John growled, disturbed by the noise and John's presence, and came closer. "Buzz off," hissed John, turning to it for a moment. It was such a small dog, no one could take its threats seriously. Even the dog seemed aware of its impotence. Still, it had a strong sense of property. What was this stranger doing here?

"And now, for this morning's bulletin," said Father Fabiano. He took an age to adjust a pair of spectacles and then raised the telegram. "Here is the text of Silvestro's message word for word. 'Beloved fellow Roccaspartians, life is a complex of misery and hope, and we live between the two. One moment we are rich and the next moment poor. One moment down-hearted and the next raised to glorious heights. It is, as I well know, a gamble—' "

"The news, father, please!" A wail went up.

Father Fabiano shook his head. "Patience." And then went on, "'Last night I fought for the town of my birth. And now my heart is sad. You will never see me again for my heart is heavy with the shame of defeat. All was lost, even to the last lire, on a desperate throw. Farewell, Silvestro.' "

For a moment there was dead silence in the square. John found himself thinking that Silvestro must have saved over a few lire in order to pay for such a long telegram. Then there came a burst of angry voices, disappointed cries and a weird banshee howl from the lustier spirits in the crowd. The Goldini bath was lost. The prosperity of Roccasparta was now a thing of the past. The noise went up in a great gust of sound that made the pigeons around the church façade take to the air in a great confusion of wings. And the noise was John's undoing. The dog behind him, although faint-hearted, was startled into courage. It leaped forward and bit him sharply on the right ankle. John gave a cry of pain, half-turned, and then stumbled backwards and crashed through the bamboo screen to sprawl in the garden in full view of the crowd. The dog ran forward and licked his face, apologetically, but the damage was done.

"Il Canadese!"

"Ladro!"

"Stealer of Baths!"

"Villain!"

The next moment the angry crowd was advancing towards John.

He struggled to his feet, and there was no doubt in his mind that once they caught him it would take a long time for anyone to reassemble the parts. He began to run and, since his way was blocked back to the villa, he headed out across the square for the Albergo Nationale. As he reached it, with the crowd in full cry behind him, the door was slammed in his face and he heard the bolt shoot home. He turned and raced towards the far end of the square, but a section of the crowd had anticipated his move and was already moving to cut him off. He heard Rosario's voice shouting orders and he doubled back between two wings of the crowd heading for the row of trees on the church side of the square. But when he reached them, hoping for some open doorway in the houses on that side, he saw every door and window shut. Turning, panting, he watched the crowd, split into five or six sections now, and no longer running, come slowly towards him. He was trapped, and for the first time he realised that gay and light-hearted though the Italians were normally, they were quite different when they were roused and saw their livelihood being taken from them.

It was then, when he realised that he couldn't go forward or back or to the right or the left, that he decided to go up. He ran forward and jumped for the lower branches of one of the trees. He pulled himself up and began to climb. At the moment, he guessed, Father Fabiano wouldn't be able to handle the crowd ... but with luck he could sit it out until the temper of the crowd cooled.

But it showed no signs of cooling. They gathered in a wide circle round the tree and Rosario's voice barked an order. John began to dislike Rosario. Five or six men ran into a shop close to the tree and were soon back, carrying deep pannier baskets between them. The next moment a hail of soft peaches and apricots began to whistle around John. The fruit smashed through the leaves, splattered over his clothes, and he almost lost his hold and fell as he raised his hands to protect his face.

Down below the crowd danced and yelled round the tree and every able-bodied man and boy hurled peaches at John. In two minutes he was a mess of sticky yellow pulp and his temper had gone up to boiling point. Lips tight, pin-points of anger in his eyes,, he decided that he couldn't stay up here and be shot at like a guy. He must go down and smash into them …

But even as he made the first move, a change came over the crowd below. Over the noise they were making a woman's voice range out, angry with authority.

There was a sudden silence in the crowd.

John looked down and saw a little lane open through the crowd. Down it came Gabriella, a dark-haired girl, in a white summer frock, and her face was stern with anger. Deliberately she walked to the tree and then turned and faced the crowd. Into the silence her voice snapped like the sound of a whip cracking. "I want this square empty within the next twenty seconds! I give my word that the Goldini bath shall not leave Roccasparta. But if the square is not empty within twenty seconds I withdraw it. I, Gabriella Mondovi of the Goldini family of Roccasparta say this."

She stood there, scornful, imperious, and for a few seconds John realised it was touch and go. Then Rosario moved towards his hotel, and with his action the rest of the crowd slowly broke and drifted away. Within twenty seconds the square was empty. Gabriella turned and looked up at John.

"Come down," she said, "come down, you stupid Canadian!" Slowly John began to climb down.

When he reached the ground, Gabriella looked him up and down. He was in a mess. Just for a second the sternness went from her face and the hint of a smile flickered about her lips. Then she said seriously:

"You should have known better than to come up here this morning."

"I know, but there it is. Anyway, thank you very much, Gabriella. You saved me from being turned into peach preserve."

"They might have done anything. They are irresponsible over this affair. Now I suggest you go back to the villa."

"Don't worry, I will." He paused, and then went on. "But, you know," he frowned as he made his way across the square and she kept pace with him, "you gave them your word that the Goldini bath should stop here. I don't see how—"

"That's my problem. And I gave my word."

"But what do you expect me to do?"

"Just what you will do. Go ahead with your job."

"Hell … it's a mess, isn't it. Maybe I ought to chuck the whole thing."

Gabriella shook her head. "It's nice of you to say that. But you know yourself that Mr. Fuller would only send someone else. My uncle means to sell the bath. He needs the money."

At the top of the hill leading down to the villa Gabriella stopped. "You will be quite safe from here. I must go back to talk to Rosario. I should think Father Fabiano will be talking to him, too."

She turned and walked off and he watched her go, the skirts of her white dress swinging. There was a girl, he thought; a real girl, the kind of girl a man could … Well, she was something you didn't meet every day. It was a pity about her promise over the bath, though. He didn't see how she could stop him taking it now.

A trio of wasps began to buzz round him, attracted by the peach pulp, and he hurried on to the villa.

He bathed and put on fresh clothes and then went down to see the Count. He didn't know what Gabriella's plans might be, but he realised that his best bet was to get the bath out of Roccasparta as fast as possible.

The Count was in a small workshop at the back of the villa. He was in his shirt-sleeves and Monsieur Castillot was with him, and the Count was explaining the working of a small wooden model on a table.

"You see, my dear Castillot, if you are going to keep chicken on a large scale the question of labour becomes important. Now what is the biggest labour item ..."

"Picking up eggs, perhaps?" suggested Monsieur Castillot.

"No, no—these chicken are cockerels for table birds. No eggs. Food and drink is the problem. Now with this model, you will see that I have devised an automatic food hopper which is worked by hydraulic power ... and the hydraulic power is in fact also the drinking water. It is so simple. Michelangelo might have thought of it... Ha, here is Signore Mallet. You have come, no doubt, to present me with Mr. Fuller's cheque for the bath?"

"You know that Silvestro's lost everything?" questioned John.

"Monsieur Castillot has informed me of that. And also," for a moment the Count's eyes twinkled, "that you were for a while in quite a jam yourself." He looked at Castillot smiling. "It is a pun. I have been thinking about it for some time."

"I've got the cheque," said John. "But, if you agree, I prefer to hand it over only when the bath is loaded on to the lorry. Anything might happen yet."

The Count considered this and then nodded. "Yes, you have reason."

"You are worried about Gabriella's promise," asked Monsieur Castillot.

"Frankly I am. She's a girl who means what she says."

Castillot shook his head. "She is running her head against a brick wall. You have the necessary tools for dismantling the bath?"

"Yes."

"Then I suggest you begin work right away. When you are ready the Count and I will find help to carry it down to the lorry and you will be away before Gabriella can do anything. Speed is the important thing …" He paused and his plump genial face was suddenly sad. "It is a pity though … No Goldini bath … We shall have to delete Roccasparta from the next edition of our guide book."

"It must build a new future for itself. As I propose to do," said the Count. "We cannot live upon the past." He turned to the model. "Now also we have the problem of lighting these rearing houses, for the birds must be encouraged to eat twenty-four hours a day. For that, I have devised a system of flashing bulbs …"

But John did not stop to listen. He went off to get his tools, and he carried with him the impression that underneath his charm Count Goldini was a man with an unblinking eye for realism and facts. Still, that wouldn't butter any bread in Roccasparta.

He worked until lunchtime by himself in the bathroom. And after lunch when the rest of the villa had retired for its usual siesta he went on with the job. He was a quick, expert worker and this was a simple plumbing job … Not really the kind of job for a highly qualified engineer. But then, if you wanted to get on you turned your hand to anything. And John wanted to get on. John worked happily singing gently to himself.

In an hour he had the bath disconnected from all its inlet and outlet piping and the recess mirror panels away so that it could be lifted free from its bed. He caught hold of the end and tried its weight. It came up about an inch and he guessed that it would need three men to raise it clear. It was hot in the bathroom and he straightened up, wiping his forehead. Well, in an hour he would be away. He would never see Roccasparta again … or— the thought jabbed at him—Gabriella. He pushed the thought from him. Mr. Fuller would be delighted. He'd be given some important job, and he'd go ahead to an assured future … but somehow he couldn't take a real interest in his future. There seemed to be something lacking in it.

He stood back from the bath, whistling gently to himself. The door opened quietly behind him, and the cool draught coming through made him turn.

Three men canoe into the bathroom and with them was Gabriella. One was Rosario, spectacles pushed up on to his broad forehead, the other, a smaller younger edition of Rosario, carried a shotgun, and the third was a dark, curly-headed young man, broader than he was long, a grin all over his face and a stout stick in his hand.

"If you shout," said Rosario, "regretfully, Icaro will hit you over the head with his stick."

"Not regretfully," said Icaro, the grin widening.

"And if you attempt to run when we get down to the courtyard," went on Rosario, "my son, Cosmo, will shoot you in the legs."

"Regretfully," said Cosmo.

"So be sensible," said Gabriella. "Also, too, you will hand over Mr. Fuller's cheque which I understand you have not yet given to my uncle."

John looked at them. There wasn't a thing he could do. They meant business. Then he smiled at Gabriella.

"I've got to hand it to you. Good staff work." He drew the cheque from his pocket and held it out. It was either that or be hit over the head.

Gabriella came forward and took it. Deliberately she tore it into small pieces.

"My uncle will never let the bath leave without payment. So we do not have to worry about that for a while. Now, you will please go down into the courtyard and enter the small car which is there. And no noise."

Obediently John went down to the courtyard. Gabriella had chosen her moment well... It was the siesta hour and no one was stirring.

The car was a small Citroen and John was wedged in the back seat between Icaro and Cosmo. Rosario sat in front with Gabriella who was driving.

"Blindfold him," said Gabriella.

"Is that necessary?" asked John.

"If the Signorina says so——yes," said Icaro firmly and he whipped out a piece of dirty sacking and tied it around John's head.

"Leave him room to breathe," said Rosario.

"Regretfully, yes," said Icaro.

The car started and John felt it turn left-handed out of the villa gates and down the hill away from Roccasparta. After that he soon lost his sense of direction. On one side of him Cosmo whistled gently and on the other Icaro lit a pipe and the car filled with the odour of something that smelt like burning heather. It got hotter and hotter and John was glad that he was only wearing light drill trousers and an open-necked shirt.

After about half-an-hour of bouncing over rough country roads the car stopped. John was hustled out and the sack taken from his head. He was standing in the cool shade of a beech tree at the foot of a long hill slope covered with myrtle bushes and dwarf oaks.

"From here," said Gabriella, "it does not matter what you see."

John smiled. She sounded crisp, full of authority; the general in charge of an important operation. They started up the slope, Gabriella and Rosario leading, then John and Icaro and Cosmo bringing up the rear. They did about three miles, climbing all the time towards the distant flat crest of a block of hills. John tried to remember his map ... but there were so many hills around Roccasparta that this might have been any of them. At one point the hillside was broken by a long shelving ridge with a steep slope of boulders and loose stones. The path disappeared and they had to scramble up a steep climb, little lizards flashing in and out of the hot stones as they went. Beyond the ridge the ground levelled off for a while across tufty, dry marsh-land and then gave way to a thick belt of pines and spruce.

When they came out of the trees, there, facing them was a small cottage set back into a notch of the hillside. There was only one floor. Yellow maize cobs hung drying in a long freize from the roof edge and a few hens pecked about the open doorway.

"It is," said Rosario proudly, "my shooting box. Up here there are many quail."

John was ushered into the house. It consisted of two large rooms; one which opened off the main door, and another leading from the main room.

"Take him into the other room," said Gabriella, "and remove all his clothes, except his underpants." She turned to John. "It is necessary in case you think of escaping."

"I do think of escaping, believe me!"

"Then you will have a long way to go bare-footed and in your pants."

"You're crazy!" His temper was now a little frayed with the hot ride and the long climb. "What do you think you're going to achieve?"

Gabriella ignored him. "Rosario and you, Icaro—you will stay with him for the first week. After that we will change the guards round each week—"

"Hey, what's this?" demanded John indignantly. "How long do you think you're going to keep me here?"

Cosmo looked at him sadly, "But until all the tickets are sold, signore. It may take six weeks."

"What tickets? What is this?"

Gabriella was silent for a moment, and then with a judicial nod of her head that shook the loose dark hair around her neck, she said, "Perhaps it is fair that you should know. Since Silvestro has failed, we have thought of another way of raising the money. We are going to start a lottery all over Italy. The first prize will be five million lire, the second two million and the third a million. That means we have to sell twenty-three million lire's worth of tickets. We shall have fifteen million left over to buy the bath. But, of course it will take a long time—"

"You're telling me!" John almost shouted. "And you think I'm going to stay here all that time?"

"You have no choice. You will be fed, of course," explained Rosario.

"And given a change of underclothes now and again," said Cosmo.

"Well, that's something. Thanks. But—" John faced Gabriella, "—what do you think Fuller's going to do? When he learns I've disappeared he'll only send someone else with a cheque for the Count."

"Then we shall kidnap him," said Icaro grinning. "It is simple."

"And if he sends another," explained Cosmo quietly, "then we shall kidnap him."

"I see. Well …" John shrugged his shoulders, "… in time I can see I'm going to have enough company to make up a bridge four."

Gabriella began to laugh and then cut it short. "Into the other room with him."

The three men closed in on John and he was crowded into the other room. It had a bed, two chairs and a table, and the tiny window was barred. When they left he had nothing but his underpants. The bolts of the communicating door clanged home. Then, almost immediately, they were clanged back and the door opened. Gabriella's head appeared for a moment round the edge and, seeing him sitting on the bed, she smiled and said apologetically, "Please, do not be too angry. I must do this for the people of Roccasparta. We shall try to make you as comfortable as possible." She tossed a packet of cigarettes and a box of matches to him and then her head withdrew and he heard the bolts go home again.

And that was that. The Great Goldini Bath Lottery. How long did they think that would really take them? At, say, twenty lire a ticket … He began to work out how many people would have to buy tickets, but gave it up. Gabriella was slipping, too, he told himself. She hadn't tried to sell him a ticket … Suddenly he smiled. The girl was crazy. This whole idea of a lottery was impractical. She'd never sell that number of tickets. And did they really think they could keep him prisoner all that time? Not if he knew it. Still, he had to admire her. She made up her mind—no matter how fantastic her plan might be—and then went into action.

He got up and tried the bars of the little window. They were set tight in the surrounding masonry.

Outside, in the other room, he could hear Rosario and Icaro talking. Towards evening, the bolts were drawn back and Rosario came in to bring him food and wine.

"Do not try to do anything, for Icaro sits outside with a shotgun," warned Rosario. He set the meal down on the table and withdrew.

Darkness carne and eventually John flung himself down on the bed. But is was a long time before he slept. He was thinking, and frowning furiously into the dark.

The next day Rosario brought him his breakfast, and for ten minutes, while the men flanked him with a shotgun each he was allowed to take a little exercise around the house.

Rosario brought him lunch and for the rest of the afternoon John lay on the bed, planning how he would receive Rosario when he came in with dinner. He was getting out of here, even if it meant having his skin peppered with small shot …

Fifteen minutes before Rosario was due with his supper, John lay on the bed watching the door. It seemed ages before he heard the sound of the bolts being drawn. Rosario came in, spectacles pushed up on to his forehead, and carrying a small tray. He nodded to John and theca set the tray down on the table. Just for a second his back was turned to John.

John twisted silently off the bed and his left hand grabbed the heavy quilt. In one swift moment he flung it over Rosario's head and muffled it around his face. He pushed Rosario back onto the bed and held him there, face pressed on to the bed by one hand, while with the other he worked off the man's jacket; and then sitting astride of him, he pulled off the loose sandals he wore. Rosario's feet beat up and down on the soft bed but made no noise.

Then John slid off the bed, pulled up all the clothes he could and piled them over Rosario who, half-suffocated now, was struggling no more. John sat on the lump of clothes and pulled on the jacket and sandals.

He got up and went swiftly to the door. As he walked through into the next room there came a long, gurgling cry from behind him. The noise made Icaro, who was standing by the table in the outer room, look round. His mouth dropped open in surprise and then, coming to his senses, he made a grab for the shot gun which rested on the table. John jumped for him and his right fist swung forward, taking Icaro on the point of the chin.

The man crashed backwards across the table and John sprinted for the open door. As he did so, he saw from the corner of his eye his own trousers resting across the back of a chair. He swept them up in passing and the next moment was racing for the line of dark pine trees. Behind him the cottage rang with shouts and cries and then, suddenly, the evening was split with the bursting noise of a shotgun being fired. A hail of pellets whipped through the air to John's right and peppered the trunks and foliage of the pines.

John raced into the trees, and went straight down the path for twenty yards, then he swung away right-handed, heading for the thickest part of the wood. In five minutes the sound of his pursuers behind him died away. He stopped and quickly pulled on his trousers and then headed away through the wood.

When he came to the edge of the wood he looked carefully across the open stretch of dry dusk-shadowed marshland. There was no sign of anyone. John moved out into the open and began to trot towards the steep ridge that barred the way down the hill slope. If he could reach the road where he had left the car he was pretty sure that eventually he could make his way back to the Villa Goldini. And this time he'd take care that there was no kidnapping. Mr. Fuller was going to get his bath.

The evening dusk was thickening now. He came to the edge of the ridge, but just as he reached it a figure came toiling over it and was silhouetted against the distant sky.

Momentarily there was only five yards between them. John was facing Gabriella. She had a shotgun under her arm and was wearing trousers and a short leather jacket.

He swore to himself and swung off to the right, running hard along the top of the ridge. Gabriella gave a cry behind him and then he heard her running after him. He kept on, knowing that if she got a chance of a good shot she would fire at his legs. The thought made him so uncomfortable that he turned and went down over the edge of the ridge. It was steep and dangerous with loose stones. But he ploughed down, leaping and sliding, grabbing at the small bushes for support. Behind him he heard the slithering sound of stones as Gabriella followed. He was almost at the bottom when he heard her cry out. But there was something about the cry which made him brake and halt. This wasn't the cry of a pursuer. It was a woman calling out in a moment of fear.

The next instant there was an ominous rush of stones, another cry and a small avalanche of debris swept down to him from the gloom and he saw Gabriella's body come sliding along the top. He flung himself forward and grabbed at her. But he missed her and was carried forward with the loose slide of stones. He did the last five yards flat on his back and lay for a moment winded. Then to his right he heard the sound of heavy breathing. He struggled up and moved across the loose rocks.

Gabriella lay on her side, wedged between two stout myrtle bushes. He bent down quickly and pulled her free. She lay in his arms, breathing with a quick little pulse of noise as though she were having an unpleasant dream, and her eyes were shut. There was a large bruise on one of her temples.

He shook her gently and called to her but her eyes remained shut. It was quite clear what had happened. She had slipped while chasing after him and her head must have hit a rock or bush stump and she had been knocked out.

He knew he could never carry her up the ridge slope. Then he remembered that at the foot of the slope there was a small stream. Full of anxiety, he picked her up in his arms and began to carry her down the slope. After a while he found the stream and laid her down on the grass. He took off Rosario's jacket and folded it under her head. He went to the stream, wetted his handkerchief and came back to bathe her forehead. She still breathed curiously and her eyes were shut.

It was twenty minutes before she came round, and they were the worst twenty minutes in his life. He sat there not knowing what to do except keep on bathing her forehead and splashing water on her face. And then when he was debating whether he should leave her here and get help or carry her down to the road and find her car, her eyes flickered open in the dusk and in a rather tired voice she said, "That's enough water. You're soaking my blouse."

"Gabriella …" He wanted to grab her in his arms and hug her to him in his relief. Then he held back. After all she might have broken a rib or something.

"Don't move,' he said. "Maybe you've broken something."

She sat up gingerly and felt herself. "No, I'm all right. It was just the crack on the head." Then a frown coming over her face, she said, "What are you doing here?"

John smiled. "Escaping, of course."

"I know," she answered. "But I thought you must have got away this morning. I thought that was what it meant."

"What what meant?" asked John, puzzled.

"The lorry, of course."

"Look, Gabriella, h don't know what you're talking about. What lorry? Why don't you tell it straight?"

For a moment she was silent, thinking. Then she said, "This is very odd, I don't know what's happened then." She looked at, him perplexed, and then said, "Perhaps my head isn't clear yet. Have you got a cigarette?"

"Sorry, I carne away in a hurry. Perhaps there are some in Rosario's jacket." He reached out for the jacket and felt in the pockets. There was a rattle of matches from one of them and he pulled out a mass of stuff, cigarettes, matches, a crumpled hotel menu, some keys and a battered wallet. The wallet fell to the ground at his feet.

He lit a cigarette and handed it to her. She drew on it gratefully.

"Now tell me what's happened," he said.

"Well, during the siesta hour this afternoon, your lorry disappeared from the villa courtyard—and the bath has gone also."

John, who had just struck a match to light himself a cigarette, paused in surprise. "The bath's gone! Who the devil could have taken it?" He frowned, staring before him, the match flame flickering gently in the evening air.

"Well, I thought it might be you. That's why I came hurrying out here, to make sure."

"Me? No ... Damn!" The burning match-end singed his fingers and he flung it away. He struck another to light his cigarette and, as he bent forward to the flame, he noticed something white lying on the ground before him. He paused, and then held the match a little lower. Under the light of the-match two faces stared up at him from a photograph on the ground. Distantly in his mind a warning bell began to ring.

He reached forward and picked up a battered postcard-size photograph which had slipped out of Rosario's wallet. He held the match closer to it, and then he whistled in surprise.

"This is no time to go through other people's wallets," said Gabriella impatiently. "Don't you understand? The bath has gone. That means neither Mr. Fuller nor Roccasparta will get it. It's been stolen."

"Sure," said John absently. "Sure." But his attention was on the card. It was a photograph of two men in their Sunday best, taken outside the Albergo Nationale. One of the men was Rosario, spectacles pushed up, and the other—John had no doubt of it— was the man he had seen drunk in the little lakeside cabin on the evening of his first arrival in Roccasparta. But more significant than anything else was the inscription scrawled across the bottom of the card—*Me and my cousin Silvestro*.

"What is the matter with you?" asked Gabriella.

"Look." John struck another match, and held the card towards her., covering the inscription. "Who's this man on the right?"

"It's Silvestro, of course. But what has this—"

"Listen," said John. "I saw this man Silvestro, drunk in a little cabin by the side of Lago di Nello, the first night I arrived here."

"But you couldn't have done. He was away at the Casino gambling to make the bath money."

"He couldn't have been. He was at Lago di Nello."

"What are you suggesting?"

"Well—somebody's got the bath. Silvestro was a gangster in America. Just suppose, for instance, that Silvestro and, say, a couple of accomplices decided that they would like the bath."

"Silvestro wouldn't do a thing like that."

"Some men will do anything. An accomplice could have sent false messages from the Casino to string everyone along. And Silvestro could have waited around here, hidden up, until I'd got the bath out of the villa and on to the lorry. Then it could have been stolen from me as I drove off. But as it happened they didn't have to do that. I was kidnapped and the bath was left dismantled, ready for anyone to pick up."

"I don't believe it."

"The bath's gone, isn't it?"

"But what would Silvestro do with the bath? You couldn't smuggle it out of the country as it is—Oh …" Gabriella gave a sudden little cry of alarm.

"Yes," said John, putting his hand on her arm gently. "That's it. They'd have to melt it down. You can smuggle out odd-sized chunks of gold."

"But where would they do that? It's a big job."

"Of course, it is. You'd want time and no interruptions. I may be wrong, but I've got a feeling that Silvestro decided that the Lago di Nello was just the place where he could work in peace. Why else should he have been hiding out there when he should have been at the Casino? I think we ought to go and have a look."

He stood up. "How do you feel? Fit enough for a long walk?"

"I'm all right, but …"

John reached down his hand and helped her up. "I know you can't believe Silvestro would do this. But let's give it a try."

"Where are we going?"

"To Lago di Nello. How far is it?"

"About four miles."

"You feel strong enough to make it?"

"Of course, I do. It was only a little bump on the head."

"Let's go then. No time to lose—"

John began to move off, holding her hand. Then he paused, turned to her and pulled her into his arms and kissed her quickly "I meant to do that while you were unconscious," he said as he stepped back from an astonished Gabriella, "but I thought it would be taking an unfair advantage."

Before she could reply he was heading off into the darkness holding her hand.

It was nearly mid-night when they reached the Lago di Nello. Now and again a little slip of a moon showed through the low-lying clouds and there was an occasioned scud of rain. They came down through the quarry where John had spent the night and made their way to the roadside by the lake.

John made Gabriella wait a few yards away while he crept forward and examined the small but where he had seen Silvestro. When lie came back he said to Gabriella, "It's empty."

Gabriella was silent for a moment. Then she reached out and took his arm and said, "Come with me."

She began to lead him towards the lakeside.

"What's in your mind?' John asked.

"Well, if Silvestro really did take the bath and meant to melt it down, he wouldn't risk it in that hut. It's too near the road. Anyone might see him. He'd want somewhere safer than that. I know this lake. Right out in the middle there's a little treecovered island and a small cottage that the duck-hunters use in the winter. He'll be out there if anywhere."

"And how do we get out there? Swim?"

"No. There are some duck-punts and a skiff … This way." She worked her way forward through the scrub round the edge of the lake and finally they came to a ricketty wooden jetty built out over the water. In the passing light of the moon John saw a collection of punts tied alongside, and a small skiff. He pulled the skiff in and held it while Gabriella got aboard.

Following her directions he began to row quietly out towards the centre of the lake. Gabriella sat in the stern nursing the shotgun in her arms. Once they ran into a low bank of reedcovered sand, and he had to back away from it.

"The lake is slowly silting up," whispered Gabriella. "There are sandbanks and reed patches everywhere."

John said, "You are the most beautiful, intelligent, sensitive girl in the world, and I love you."

"Pull more on your left oar," she said.

"When we are married, do you think I could get a job in Rome? Or would you prefer to live in Canada? That's if Mr. Fuller will ever let me go back."

"You think too much about what Mr. Fuller will do."

"No … the only thing I've got on my mind is you. If you won't marry me, I shall shoot myself."

"Well, you can't do it here. It would make too much noise. Careful now … We're almost there."

John gave up and, under her direction, eased the boat gently towards the shadowy bulk of the little island which now began to loom up. The nose of the skiff grated softly on sand and John stepped over the side. He reached out and helped Gabriella ashore and then took the shotgun from her.

Somewhere out on the lake a wild-fowl called eerily, and overhead a plane droned by, its navigation lights winking … heading for Rome, thought John … and for a moment he pictured himself in Rome with Gabriella.

Her voice came softly to him, "Follow me and watch the path for tree roots." Her warm hand took his and they began to steal forward. The wind soughed through the trees over their heads and the darkness of the little wood closed around them.

After a few moments Gabriella halted. Ahead of them a small light was showing through the tree.

"From the cottage," she whispered.

John went ahead and she followed. In front of the cottage was a cleared space with a small wooden palisade and an open gate. The light came from a window to the left of the door. John crossed the grass to it and looked in. At his side he could hear Gabriella's soft breathing.

Together they stared through the window. "Silvestro," Gabriella whispered.

And it was Silvestro. He was sitting at a wooden table with a pack of cards in his hands, playing patience. There was a bottle of wine and a glass at his side, and over the table hung a small oil lamp. Silvestro was in his shirt sleeves, and there was a frown on his face as he laid out the cards. Now and again he paused and rubbed his neat little moustache thoughtfully. Once he reached forward and turned up the edge of a card and a smile split his face, showing the flash of his gold teeth.

"Can't even play patience without cheating," murmured John. "Leave this to me. There doesn't seem to be anyone else there."

He moved back to the door and Gabriella followed him.

"Ready?" For a moment his hand touched hers.

Then he reached forward, jerked open the door, and stepped into the room. Gabriella followed him and shut it behind her. For a moment the flame of the oil lamp guttered in the sudden draught and the room was almost in darkness. Then the light came up strongly.

Silvestro looked tip at John, open-mouthed, and then began to rise.

"Sit where you are," snapped John and the shotgun carne up threateningly.

Silvestro subsided into his chair. "*Mamma mia, signore,*" he breathed. "You should knock before you come in. To burst in like that is enough to give a man heart-failure ... And please to point that gun somewhere else."

Gabriella came forward into the light.

"Silvestro," she said sternly, "what are you doing here? And where is the bath?"

A broad smile broke across Silvestro's face, "What happiness ... it is the beautiful Signorina Gabriella. But signorina, you know as well as I do that this is a simple hunter's cabin. One cannot get a bath here ..." He laughed, but there was a note of falseness in it.

"O.K. Silvestro," said John, "now you've got over your surprise, let's get down to facts. You know what Signorina Gabriella means. The Goldini bath. The one you swiped from the villa. Where is it?"

Silvestro looked at Gabriella. "Who is this gentleman?"

"Answer the question," said Gabriella. "Where is the bath?"

"But there is no bath," Silvestro spread his pudgy hands in a puzzled gesture.

"Why are you here, anyway," demanded John. "Your last telegram said that Roccasparta would never see you again."

"Ah, Signore ... in one's grief one says many things. But at heart I am true Roccaspartian ... I come back here for a while. Tomorrow, the next day, I go to Roccasparta. Yes, I am pure Roccaspartian and cannot say goodbye without one last visit."

"You're pure villain—"

"Really, signore—" began Silvestro indignantly.

"Cut it out. You were here a week ago, when you were supposed to be at the Casino. I saw you ... Here," John handed the shotgun to Gabriella. "You keep him covered while I have a look round."

Gabriella took the shotgun and kept Silvestro covered.

John crossed the room and pushed open a door that led into the back of the cottage. One look told him all he wanted to know. Against the wall was a workbench with a vize and various tools, and beyond it a small furnace with a pin-point of red-hot charcoal burning in it and a pair of leather bellows underneath to be operated by foot. But there was no sign of the bath.

He went back into the main room.

"He's got everything in there for breaking it up. Now come on, Silvestro ... where's the bath?"

"I know nothing of any bath."

"What do I do?" John asked Gabriella. "Beat him about the head until he decides to tell the truth?"

Silvestro shook his head and then appealed to Gabriella, "Signorina ... it is as I say, I know nothing of the bath. I come back here for a last visit to Roccasparta. Also, I guess, this is the young Canadian who comes to take the bath away from Roccasparta. I am sad that you should be helping him to find the bath in order to take it away—"

"You know the bath's gone, then?" said Gabriella.

"But, of course, signorina. You have told me. It is a great shock."

"We're wasting our time," said John impatiently. "All that stuff in the other room shows quite clearly the bath is going to be broken up here. But it isn't here yet. Why not? Because obviously Silvestro has accomplices who took it off in the lorry. They're laying a false trail in the lorry, maybe switching the bath to another vehicle, and then coming back here to do the job—"

"*Mon ami*," said a quiet voice from the door, "that is an excellent piece of deduction."

Both Gabriella and John swung round at the interruption. As they did so two men stepped in through the door and one of them twisted the shotgun from Gabriella's hands before she knew what was happening. He stepped back levelling it at them. He was a lean, rangy-looking man in a peaked cap and chauffeur's breeches. At his side stood Monsieur Castillot, and he held a nasty-looking little automatic in his hand. With the other he swept off his hat and gave them a low bow. Momentarily his bald head shone under the oil light.

"Yes, *mon ami*," said Monsieur Castillot pleasantly, "an excellent piece of deduction. But you arrived at it—fortunately for us—a trifle late. Silvestro," he frowned, "stand up when in the presence of a lady." As Silvestro rose to his feet Monsieur Castillot gave Gabriella a wave of his hand and said, "Signorina, please sit down."

Without a word Gabriella sat at the table and John moved to her side. Monsieur Castillot nodded approvingly and then with a tip of his head towards the man with a shotgun added, "I am not sure whether you have met my chauffeur, Anatol … He is an extremely capable man, but a little impetuous. Please do not make him fidgetty by any unexpected movement."

"I'm beginning," said John grimly, "to see daylight."

"If you try anything funny, you'll never see real daylight again," said Anatol.

Monsieur Castillot waved a placatory hand. "Now, Anatol. These are my good friends. There is no need to be rude."

John said, "You meant to take the bath from me—if I ever got it in the lorry. You—"

"Please," Monsieur Castillot looked shocked for a moment. "Don't let us indulge in personalities. I have long had my eye on the bath. Your coming was a great help to us."

Gabriella said, "Monsieur Castillot—you can't seriously be thinking of breaking up the bath. You're a man who has a great love of beauty, and the Goldini bath …"

"Unfortunately, signorina, I also have a great love of money. How else can I get the bath out of Italy and also show a profit? Yes, yes, I love beauty but also a fat bank balance. Being the editor of a series of guide books, you know, gives me a wonderful opportunity to examine beautiful things and sometimes in one way or another to acquire them."

"And what do you propose to do with us?" asked John sharply.

Monsieur Castillot smiled. "Nothing violent, if that's what you mean. No, we shall just keep you here until our work is finished. When we leave we shall make sure that you cannot escape for a few days. After that—well, the world is wide and we have many places to go to. It is, you think, a friendly, sensible arrangement?"

"I'd like to knock your heads off," snorted John.

"But, of course. That is an inevitable reaction, and I forgive it." Monsieur Castillot giggled gently.

"We've got work to do," said Anatol impatiently.

"*Si, si* ..." agreed Silvestro. "But what of these two?"

"Over the next room," said Monsieur Castillot, "there is, I seem to remember, a little loft without windows. They can be put there for the time being. If I am not mistaken, they will not object to each other's company. I have watched the signs with great pleasure. After beauty and money what is there more enchanting than *l'amour*?"

"You talk too much," said Anatole crisply. "We should shoot them and throw them in the lake."

"No," said Silvestro contemptuously, "it is crude and unnecessary. Even in America we would not do such a thing. I remember a similar situation in Chicago—"

"There is no need to labour the point, Silvestro," said Monsieur Castillot. "We have the bath in the punt now and shall need your help to get it up here. But first let us see our friends safely locked away."

John looked down at Gabriella. For a moment their eyes met and he saw the corners of her mouth tremble. But he knew that it was not from fear but from frustration at their own helplessness and the thought of what was going to happen to the Goldini bath. In that moment his love for her became something real and solid. And like any young man in love who sees the shadowy tears of disappointment and sadness in his love's eyes, John was suddenly grimly determined that Gabriella should be made happy.

Ignoring the other men, he said to her quietly, "Gabriella—from this moment I am no longer employed by Mr. Fuller. I'm on your side and, if it's the last thing I do, I'll see that Roccasparta keeps its bath."

"A noble, knightly speech," said Monsieur Castillot, sighing sentimentally. "And now to the loft—"

"To the bath!" shouted John and with his cry he swung his right hand out and smashed at the hanging oil lamp. With the other he pulled Gabriella up and pushed her through the sudden darkness towards the door of the cabin.

There was a high cry of alarm from Monsieur Castillot. Someone reached out in the darkness and caught John's collar. He smacked out and had the satisfaction of feeling his fist strike flesh. Somebody gave a grunt of pain and a chair crashed to the ground. Ahead of him John saw

Gabriella's silhouette against the door and then a darker shape swept between it and him. He lowered his head and charged. Somebody went down before him. He felt his feet pound across a body and then he was out in the open. A shotgun went off close behind him and the pellets whipped against the leaves of the trees above his head. Monsieur Castillot's voice screamed, "Stop firing, you fool!"

Then John was pounding down the little path, hearing Gabriella ahead of him and the noise of pursuit close behind. It was a nightmare run. Twice John tripped over tree roots and went flying full length. Winded he pulled himself up and ran on. Once, as the moon whipped from behind a cloud he saw Gabriella ahead. Then the darkness gathered rapidly round him again. From behind came the shouts of Anatol and Silvestro. Suddenly John was out of the trees, his feet sliding on soft sand. "This way!" Gabriella's voice called to him from the darkness. He raced across the little beach and found her by the skiff. Drawn in beside it was a large, fiat-bottomed duck-punt and in it was a long, shrouded shape.

"The bath. Get in."

John pushed Gabriella into the punt and as she stumbled forward across the bath he bent and began to push the punt outward. For a moment it stuck and would not move.

"Get up the other end. It'll free the bows," shouted John. As Gabriella moved forward, the punt came off the sand and began to move outwards. John pushed it hard, wading into a foot of water. He was just about to jump in when there was a rush of feet across the sand behind him. Two dark shapes came ploughing through the water and quick hands reached out and seized him. He was jerked backwards and the punt floated away into the darkness without him.

The next moment John was submerged by the weight of Silvestro and Anatol. They crashed down on him and the three of them collapsed in a struggling mass of arms and legs in a foot of water.

But there was a strength in John now which he had never known before. The bath was going to stay in Roccasparta. He kicked and, thrashed and hit out, swallowed water, went under and came up to strike about him like a madman. Silvestro and Anatol clung to hurl like a couple of octopuses, and somewhere in the background, he could hear the shrill voice of Monsieur Castillot crying out in exasperation and alarm.

His fist found a chin and one of the two men stumbled back from him. Sobbing for breath John bent forward and flung the other man over his shoulders like a sack of potatoes. There was a great splash of water. John threw himself outwards, swam a few strokes and then went under, swimming below the surface as long as he could.

He came to the top in the darkness and trod water gently. Thirty yards away, from the shore, came the sound of the three men shouting and swearing.

John swam on quietly. When he was some way out he slipped off Rosario's jacket to give him greater freedom. He looked up at the sky. A great pall of cloud streamed before the wind and, briefly, the moon came through a ragged break in the clouds. He looked across the surface of the water. Just for a moment he caught the dark shape of a punt a hundred yards from .him. Then the moon went.

He began to swim towards it, calling gently to Gabriella. In a few moments he had reached the punt and Gabriella was helping him inboard. Once aboard he sat for a while, getting his breath back.

"You're all right?" whispered Gabriella.

"Sure …"

"What do we do now?"

"Paddle on a bit. But keep it as quiet as you can—and don't head for the jetty. I've got to think this one out."

Gabriella swung the punt round and headed quietly for the far end of the lake and away from the roadside.

After awhile John said, "O.K., stop paddling."

They drifted gently through the darkness.

"You were magnificent," said Gabriella. "I've got a feeling that perhaps I do love you …"

John reached out and took one of her hands and kissed it softly.

They sat there in silence for a while. Then across the waters came the sound of the splashing of oars.

"They're out in the skiff looking for us," said John. He took the paddle from Gabriella and edged the punt forward quietly towards a patch of reeds that loomed in the darkness. The punt rustled into the shelter of the reeds.

"They'll go on looking until they find us," said Gabriella.

"They want the bath not us. If we swam ashore and left it here, by the time we got back with help they would have found it and gone. Monsieur Castillot's no fool. He'd load it up on whatever transport they've got by the jetty and be miles away—" John broke off and put his hand out quickly and held Gabriella's arm.

Not far away the water was disturbed by the beat of oars and the dark shape of the skiff passed within a few yards.

When it was gone Gabriella said, "But there seemed to be only one man in it, John."

"I know. Listen."

Distantly over the water came the sound of the lift and drop of paddles and now and again the low calling of voices. "They've got out a couple of punts from the jetty and now all three are after us, each in a different boat. They'll comb the lake from end to end. Monsieur Castillot knows we can't risk abandoning the bath. Even if they don't find us in the dark, when daylight comes we'll be sunk,"

John was silent for a while. Over the lake water came the sound of their searchers, the quiet dip and splash of paddles and oars and the low calling of voices.

Suddenly John said, "But that's it! I've just given myself the answer. What a fool not to think of it before! Come on, we've got work to do!"

He grabbed the paddle and began to ease the punt out of the reeds.

"Where are we going?" asked Gabriella puzzled.

John handled her the paddle. "Keep heading for the jetty, but make it soft and slow. You say this lake is silting up?"

"Yes."

"How deep is it on an average?"

"Not more than five or six feet anywhere. Shallower by the jetty."

"That's it then. It came to me when I said we'd be sunk. We'll sink the punt with the bath in it. Can't hurt the bath and it can be picked up anytime. Meanwhile we go off and get help—"

"John, what a wonderful idea."

"I'm full of them."

As he spoke John began to grope around the floor boards of the punt, looking for the bilge plug. He found it, a large cork from a wine flask rammed tight into a hole in one of the planks. He worked it loose and pulled it half out. Dark water began to seep through and across the boards.

"O.K." he said. "Stop paddling as soon as she begins to sink and we'll swim quietly off." They were nearing the jetty now and could see its straddling shape silhouetted against the sky. Behind them came still the sounds of calling voices and the steady beat of oars.

John pulled the plug right out and the water poured into the punt. It crept up the freeboard and the punt began to settle, the weight of the bath sinking it down evenly and steadily.

Slowly it filled and then one end tipped gently and the lake water rolled in. The next moment the punt was under and still sinking. John and Gabriella stood up, the water to their knees and still rising as they sank, and then they swam off. With quiet strokes they made their way to the shore about fifty yards below the jetty.

They waded out and into the cover of the trees where they wrung the water from their clothes as best they could. As they stood there in the darkness, John reached out and pulled the damp form of Gabriella to him.

"Up to now," he said quietly, "I've had too much on my mind to give attention to the really important thing."

He pulled her closer, felt her arms go round his neck and his lips found hers. For a while there was only the sound of the breeze in the trees, the pale slip of moon sliding out of the clouds now and then and the steady drip of water from their clothes.

Drawing away from John, Gabriella said, "And now what, darling?"

"We get married, of course," said John.

"No, I mean about the bath."

"We go back to Roccasparta and get— Listen!"

John's hand went out and held Gabriella's arm. Not far out on the lake came the sound of a boat moving. They turned watching the dark waters. A punt was coming in. They could hear a man breathing and panting. A dark shape detached itself from the gloom and the next moment, not ten yards from them, a punt was driven up on to the strip of foreshore. A short, plumpish man got out, reached down into the punt and lifted out a bulky object and then turned and headed away from them towards the lake road.

"Silvestro," whispered Gabriella. "What's he up to?"

"He's a wise rogue," murmured John. "It's my bet he knows when the time comes to abandon ship. If I know Silvestro he's making off and leaving the others to look after themselves. I wonder what that is he's carrying? Looks like a hand-grip."

"We ought to stop him."

"We're going to."

John began to move off after Silvestro with Gabriella following him.

Silvestro made his way through the trees towards the jetty. John and Gabriella kept about fifty yards behind him. On the road. running out to the jetty a strange lorry was parked in the shadow of the trees. It wasn't John's lorry and he guessed they must have switched over somewhere to cover their traces.

To John's surprise Silvestro ignored the lorry and hurried by it, keeping to the road. A couple of hundred yards further along the road he turned off into the trees. John and Gabriella stopped. A few moments later, they heard the quiet sound of a motor starting and being kept down at very low throttle. A small black shape suddenly broke away from the mass of tree shadows and slid out on to the road.

"Come on!" urged John.

He began to run. He was within five yards of the car when Silvestro heard them coming. It was an open touring car and John saw the white flash of Silvestro's face as he turned his head in surprise. The car immediately began to gather speed along the road, but it was too late.

John grabbed the side and swung himself overboard into the back seat, and the next moment Gabriella had leaped to the running board and was hanging on.

John shot his hands out and grabbed Silvestro by the neck. "All right, Silvestro," he said grimly. "Take it gently until Signorina Gabriella is aboard."

Silvestro slowed the car and Gabriella climbed in alongside him.

From the back seat John, releasing his grip on Silvestro, said, "Now carry on—and head for Roccasparta. And don't try any nonsense." "*Mamma mia*," sighed Silvestro. "I wish I had stayed in America."

It was a very chastened Silvestro who drove them back to Roccasparta.

"When the people of Roccasparta know to what I have done they will lynch me," he said gloomily.

"That's right," said John cheerfully.

"Maybe, Father Fabiano will talk them out of it," said Gabriella. "Though I doubt it."

"Your sympathy, signorina, overwhelms me," said Silvestro. "Anyway, it is all Monsieur Castillot's fault. It was his idea. I wish I had never met him in Rome. He is a very bad man."

"You should be a good judge of that," said John.

"Money," said Silvestro darkly, "it is worse than love for making a man go wrong. Why did I ever leave America?"

"Probably they kicked you out," suggested John.

"Signore," said Silvestro indignantly, "who has been spreading such slander?"

"Drive into the square and stop by the church," said John. They swung into the quiet square and pulled up by the church steps. The sky was lightening and dawn was not far away.

John said, "Gabriella, you go and fetch Father Fabiano and tell him what has happened. I'll stay here and look after Silvestro." Gabriella got out and disappeared behind the church.

John sat with Silvestro. After about ten minutes, the church bell began to toll, a loud, monotonous clanging noise. The effect was magical. Windows shot up all around the square and heads poked out. Doors opened and shut with a bang and suddenly the square was alive with people. Men came running, pulling on their jackets. Women hurried out wrapping scarves around their heads. The dogs barked and the pigeons went skyward with a great clapping of wings.

In a few moments the car was surrounded. The fact that John and Silvestro were sitting in the car together obviously puzzled the crowd. There were loud greetings and cheers for Silvestro, while John received frowns and an occasional shake of a fist in his direction.

"You have caught the thief, Silvestro! Bravo!" someone shouted.

But Silvestro sat unmoved, making little response to the greetings. And then Father Fabiano and Gabriella appeared on the top of the church steps.

A silence fell on the square.

Father Fabiano said, "*Buon giorno*, my children. This morning I have very happy news for you. The bath has been found—"

A great cheer went up at this. Father Fabiano raised his hand for silence.

"But first we have work to do to bring it back. Silvestro, come up here, and you, Cosmo—" he called to Rosario's son who was in the crowd.

Silvestro got out of the car and went up the church steps. Cosmo accompanied him.

The crowd gave Silvestro another burst of cheers. But when Father Fabiano held up his hand for silence and turned to

Silvestro with a frown, the crowd sensed that something was wrong.

"To you," said Father Fabiano severely to Silvestro, "I will speak later."

"Yes, father," said Silvestro humbly.

"But for now, Cosmo—take Silvestro in the church, lock him in the vestry and keep him there until we return."

"What has Silvestro done, father?" shouted someone.

As Silvestro and Cosmo went into the church Father Fabiano turned to the crowd and began to explain very quickly what had happened. Attention came back to John and now the cheers were for him, and the crowd's anger suddenly turned towards Silvestro. Father Fabiano was explaining the operation ahead. Every vehicle that could be found would take the men of Roccasparta to Lago di Nello. Once there, one party would get to work raising the bath, and other parties would split up around the lake side to hunt for Monsieur Castillot and Anatol if they were still there.

After that things began to move. Cars, motor-cycles and bicycles were brought out. There was a honking of horns and the roaring of engines, and.in ten minutes the cavalcade was sweeping out of Roccasparta on its way to Lago di Nello.

John, driving Silvestro's car, led the way. With him were Gabriella and Father Fabiano and the local *carabiniere*. Behind them streamed the others. They roared down the hill and along the dusty roads like a great army, and every man was armed with a shotgun, a stick or a hayfork. Small boys hung on to the running boards, the dogs ran, tongues lolling out, behind them and, as they crested the hill before the drop down to the lake, the sun came up over the distant crests and shot the sky with yellow and red.

As they swung off the road on to the rough track to the jetty John saw that the lorry was still there. He drew up and jumped out. Behind him a dozen cars disgorged their occupants.

Gabriella clutched his arm and pointed out to the lake. Making its way to the jetty was the skiff with Monsieur Castillot and Anatol in it. They must have searched until daybreak for the punt with the bath and were now, too late, deciding to make their get-away.

An angry roar went up from the Roccaspartians.

The skiff swung round and headed back for the far side of the lake.

A mob of men ran for the jetty and begun to man the punts there, while other parties began of race around the lakeside to head off the skiff.

"Remember," called Father Fabiano. "No violence."

"No, no, father," called a dozen voices. And then came Rosario's voice from the crowd, "But then also there is no need to be gentle …"

"Ah … my children," sighed Father Fabiano. He turned to John. "Now, my son, show us where the bath is."

John took some men in a couple of punts and they paddled out to the spot where he had sunk the bath. From across the lake came shouts and cries and the water was churned up with the beat of paddles and oars as the hunters chased after the skiff with Monsieur Castillot and Anatol in it. The lake was large and for a time the skiff managed to evade its pursuers. But gradually it was being forced up to the far end of the lake. John saw that there was no need to worry about the skiff. Monsieur Castillot could never get away.

Two small boys stripped off and went over the side. They found the sunken punt, and then went down and fastened ropes to the bath. With two punts moored one on each side of it and the ropes firmly fastened, the bath was gently raised from the water. Its cover had floated away and it came up glistening and shining into the morning sunlight.

A great sigh of pleasure and relief went up from the salvagers. Carefully the bath was hauled aboard one of the punts and then taken back to the jetty.

Ten minutes later Monsieur Castillot and Anatol were caught and brought to the jetty.

Father Fabiano shook his head as Monsieur Castillot was escorted to him.

"Monsieur Castillot, I had great respect for you. This makes me very sad."

Monsieur Castillot shrugged his shoulders. "I am sad, too, father. But for different reasons. Still, there we are.

We must take the rough with the smooth." He smiled suddenly at John and Gabriella. "I underestimated you, Signore Mallet. That was foolish of me. I should have remembered that a young man in love is a giant ... Well, I hope you will both be happy and your future less restricted than mine appears to be going to be."

"We should have shot them as I said," growled Anatol. But no one took any notice of him, except Rosario who clouted him on the side of the head to teach him to keep a civil tongue in his mouth.

After that the procession returned to Roccasparta in triumph. The lorry with the bath in it led the way. The air rang with happy shouts, and someone made a garland of vines leaves and hung it round John's neck, and Cosmo and Rosario stood on each side of the car's running board flanking him like a couple of guards of honour.

Back at Rocasparta, the bath was lifted off the lorry and placed on the church steps. The Roccaspartians crowded round admiring it and wine and glasses were brought out. The children danced about and sang and John stood with his arm around Gabriella, happy because she was happy and the bath back in Roccasparta.

Then through the crowd came the tall, lean figure of Count Goldini. He walked up to the bath, examined it and turned to Father Fabiano, beaming.

"Not a scratch, not a mark on it, father. I am very grateful indeed to everyone. If it had been damaged then the good Mr. Fuller might not have paid me the price I needed for it—"

"Mr. Fuller!" Gabriella stepped forward angrily. "But, uncle, you can't sell it now. Not after all the trouble we've had. Why, if John and I hadn't stopped Monsieur Castillot from taking it you would have lost it for ever."

"No, it must not leave Roccasparta," shouted the crowd.

"But, Gabriella…" the Count blinked against the strong sunlight; "I have already said that I am grateful to you all. You have all done magnificently. But nothing else is altered. You know the state of my finances. I cannot go on living here. It is hard—" he looked round at the crowd. "—but what am I to do?"

"Some way must be found!" a voice called.

"Couldn't you give us more time? After all there is still the lottery idea," said Gabriella. "We could raise the money, uncle."

The Count shook his head. "I'm sorry, Gabriella, but in your heart, you know it would not work. Already I have given you all the time I can."

"That's right," said a brisk voice. in English from the crowd. "Time's precious. No more beating about the bush!"

Every head in the crowd swung round. Who was this?

John standing by Silvestro's car, turned in surprise. He knew that voice. Moving towards the bath was a short, trim figure in a panama hat and a linen suit. The man turned slightly and eyed him across the crowd. His face was red with importance and a light-coloured moustache bristled over his prim mouth. It was Mr. Fuller, his boss.

"There you are, Mallet," Mr. Fuller barked. "Fine mess you made of things! Send you up here to buy a bath. Simple operation—and you get yourself in this fix. What would happen if I gave you a real job to do?"

John was silent for a moment. Every eye in Roccasparta was on him, and although Mr. Fuller had spoken in English, there were few people there who hadn't got the gist of his words. Then John let himself go.

"If you want my advice, Mr. Fuller," John said. "You'll go and boil your head!" A wonderful sense of relief came over him as he spoke. It was worth a year's pay.

A lusty growl of approval went up from the crowd as this exchange was translated for them by Rosario and a few others. One or two bold spirits began to move towards Mr. Fuller. Seeing this Count Goldini called sharply, "Signore Fuller is my guest."

"I can look after myself!" barked Mr. Fuller. Then, moustache bristling, he turned to John.

"You're fired!" he snapped.

"You're too late, Mr. Fuller. I resigned—last night," answered John and he put his arm round Gabriella.

"John, be careful," she whispered.

"Why should I?" he said aloud. Then to Mr. Fuller he went on. "I'm sorry, but you're not going to have that bath, Mr. Fuller. It belongs to Roccasparta. It means the difference between poverty and a decent living for them."

Mr. Fuller's jaw jutted forward. "Don't ever try to get a job in Canada, young man. And I'm having the bath, even if I have to get the army, navy and police force out to take it away. Count Goldini—" he put his hand into his pocket and pulled out a thin slip of paper, "here's my cheque for fifteen million lire. The moment you accept it, I'll take full responsibility for the bath. By Jingo, it's just as I always say—never send a boy to do a man's job. Well, go on, take it." He thrust the cheque under Count Goldini's nose.

As the Count hesitated, John pushed his way through the confused crowd and stepped between Mr. Fuller and the Count. "Just a minute."

Father Fabiano touched John's arm. "No violence, my son."

John smiled "O.K. father." He turned to the Count and spoke in Italian. "You made a deal with Mr. Fuller. But you also made a deal with the people of Roccasparta. You said that if they raised the fifteen million you'd give them first claim on the bath."

"That's right."

"Then you must honour that bargain. Here, fifteen million lire. No more, no less."

As he spoke John brought up his right hand and Gabriella saw that he was holding the black hand-grip which belonged to Silvestro.

John snapped open the catch and turned the bag up over the bath. A shower of notes fell into the bath.

For a moment there was a great silence over the square. The crowd stared at the fluttering shower of notes. Then a great roar went up, and the crowd surged forward towards John, everyone wanting to shake his hand and smack him on the back. He raised his hands and fendered them off.

"Fifteen million. lire," John called to the crowd. "You raised ten thousand lire for Silvestro to gamble with. Well by a stroke of luck he turned it into fifteen million lire in a few days. But after that he kept you on a string while he and Monsieur

Castillot cooked up this idea of stealing the bath. And in the end he pretended to lose all your money, and if …"

The rest of John's words were lost in a wild outburst of shouting and cheering. The next moment the crowd had surged forward and taken hold of John. He was lifted on to stout shoulders and born aloft. Before he knew where he was, he was being swept around the square at the head of a dancing and happy procession of Roccasparta.

"*Viva Canada!*"

"*Viva John!*"

"*Viva Roccasparta!*"

"*Viva il bagno d'oro!*"

Swaying and sliding on the shoulders of the crowd, John looked back. Gabriella, smiling, was blowing kisses to him from the top of the steps. Mr. Fuller was stalking off towards the Albergo Nationale. Count Goldini was kneeling at the side of the bath carefully collecting the notes, and Father Fabiano was looking benignly out at his people.

And John hadn't a worry in the world. Even if Mr. Fuller didn't cool off the world was wide and engineers were wanted all over the place, and what did it matter where a man worked so long as the right woman was at his side?

He blew a kiss to Gabriella.

Also Available

Mr Edgar Finchley, unmarried clerk, aged 45, is told to take a holiday for the first time in his life. He decides to go to the seaside. But Fate has other plans in store…

From his abduction by a cheerful crook, to his smuggling escapade off the south coast, the timid but plucky Mr Finchley is plunged into a series of the most astonishing and extraordinary adventures.

His rural adventure takes him gradually westward through the English countryside and back, via a smuggling yacht, to London.

Mr Finchley, Book 1

OUT NOW

About the early works of Victor Canning

Victor Canning had a runaway success with his first book, *Mr Finchley Discovers his England*, published in 1934, and lost no time in writing more. Up to the start of the Second World War he wrote seven such life-affirming novels.

Following the war, Canning went on to write over fifty more novels along with an abundance of short stories, plays and TV and radio scripts, gaining sophistication and later a darker note – but perhaps losing the exuberance that is the hallmark of his early work.

Early novels and story collections by Victor Canning –

Mr Finchley Discovers His England

Mr Finchley Goes to Paris

Mr Finchley Takes the Road

Polycarp's Progress

Fly Away Paul

Matthew Silverman

Fountain Inn

The Minerva Club

The Aberdyll Onion

Young Man on a Bicycle

About the Author

Victor Canning was a prolific writer throughout his career, which began young: he had sold several short stories by the age of nineteen and his first novel, *Mr Finchley Discovers His England* (1934) was published when he was twenty-three. It proved to be a runaway bestseller. Canning also wrote for children: his trilogy The Runaways was adapted for US children's television. Canning's later thrillers were darker and more complex than his earlier work and received further critical acclaim.

Note from the Publisher

To receive background material and updates on further titles by Victor Canning, sign up at farragobooks.com/canning-signup